Tales from Devana High

Sold as Seen

Also in this series:

Concrete Chips

Tales from Devana High
Sold as Seen

Bali Rai

Hodder
Children's
Books

A division of Hodder Headline Limited

First published in 2005 by
Hodder Children's Books

A Catalogue record for this book is available from
the British Library

ISBN 0 340 87729 4

Typeset in Garamond by Avon DataSet Ltd,
Bidford-on-Avon, Warwickshire

Printed and bound in Great Britain by
Bookmarque Ltd, Croydon, Surrey

The paper and board used in this paperback are natural recyclable
products made from wood grown in sustainable forests.
The manufacturing processes conform to the environmental regulations
of the country of origin.

Hodder Children's Books
A division of Hodder Headline Limited
338 Euston Road
London NW1 3BH

*Once again to my Judgemeadow crew 1983–1988,
especially Parmy, Penny, Ben, lucy, Lisa Crouch,
Nina S, Veena, Esther, Hattie, Paul Williams,
Steve Crouch, Phil and Jez and the rest of
the little gits, Gary Belle, Gary Charles,
Hilroy Thomas, everyone in CM class over the
five years, As, and anyone else that I've not
mentioned. With big love . . .*

ONE

'Dean!'

I shot up out of bed with a jolt and shouted down to my mum that I was awake. Then I opened my bedroom door to see if the bathroom was free. It was. I picked up my towel and some underwear and ran for the shower before Ruby, my stupid sister, could get in before me. Ruby spends hours in the bathroom, doing stuff that girls do, and I had to get to school. I didn't have no time for her marathon pampering sessions. I had money to make.

'I'm off to work,' I heard my mum shout as I closed the bathroom door.

Five minutes into my shower I heard a familiar banging noise. 'Dean! Get your skinny ass outta there . . . !'

It was Ruby. I had about finished anyway but I stood under the warm spray for another five minutes just to get on her nerves. It was my purpose in life – winding her up – and I was good at it.

When I got downstairs my older brother, Gussie, was already at the table, eating his breakfast.

'Yes rude bwoi,' he said, grinning so that I could see the cornflake that was stuck to one of his teeth.

'Mornin' bro . . .' I replied, going into the kitchen to get a cup of tea and some toast.

My granddad was in there before me and he winked at me as he gave me a mug. 'Thanks, Gramps,' I said to him.

'Nuh worry yuhself, my yout' . . .' he replied in his thick Jamaican accent.

'Any chance you could make me some toast an' all?' I asked, pushing my luck.

'Ounno mek yuh own dyam toas' yuh likkle spratt,' he told me. It took me a minute but in the end I worked out that he was saying 'no'.

'OK, Gramps,' I replied, shoving two slices of toast into the machine.

'An' get yuh batty ta school, man . . .'

I told him that I was trying to do just that but he just shook his head, mumbled something that I couldn't hear and left the kitchen. The toast popped out of the machine and I grabbed it, looking for a plate.

Back in the living room I sat down at the table and spread a thick layer of butter on my bread. 'Easy with that,' Gussie told me. 'That thing there will clog up yer heart, y'know . . .'

'It's only butter, man. It's natural . . .'

'Yeah – naturally full up of *fat* . . .'

I took a big bite of toast, chewed twice and swallowed. I followed that with a giant slurp of tea.

'Since when you cared about bein' healthy?' I asked my brother.

'I been goin' to the gym in town . . . weights and that.'

'About time too, yuh fat raas . . .'

I ducked as a table mat sailed over my head, shoved the rest of the piece of toast in my mouth and chewed it down fast. When I'd finished my breakfast I left my plate on the table and went to find my rucksack, passing my sister on the way up the stairs.

'Man – that was quick. You showered *already*?' I asked her. She looked at me like I had something strange growing out of my nose.

'I just cleaned my teeth. I ain't like you,' she replied. 'How can you get yourself clean with only five minutes in the shower?'

'Is only so many times I can wash my ars—' I began.

'I don't even want to *hear* it,' Ruby replied, holding her hand in my face like those American women do on talk shows. Talk to the *hand* . . .

I found my bag in my bedroom and I ran back downstairs and into the living room.

'Who's gonna pick up your dishes after you?' asked Ruby.

I ignored her.

'You got them things for me?' I asked Gussie.

'Yeah – in that Asda bag on the sofa,' he replied.

I picked it up and looked inside where there were about thirty CDs, all of them copies.

'How much each?' I asked.

'Fiver . . . and you can keep a quid each,' he replied.

I nodded and made for the door before Ruby got out her words.

'I ain't your *slave*!' she shouted at the closed front door. Not that I heard her say it. I just knew that she would.

My brother, Gussie, is eighteen, five years older than me. He buys and sells things and works behind the bar in my dad's place. He's supposed to be getting a proper job or doing a college course but it always gets put off and my dad thinks he'll get himself sorted out when he's good and ready. I know better. Gussie is a lazy, fat git and he'll sponge off my parents for as long as he can get away with it. His full name is Augustus Pablo Chambers. He's named after one of my parents' favourite reggae artists. I could laugh at him but my full name is even worse. Dean Barrington Levy Chambers is not a name I can get on my high horse about. I'm also named after a reggae artist, as is my sister. Oh and my dad. It runs in the family, I guess. Ruby's seventeen and her middle name is Lorna, after Lorna Bennett who was a singer in the 1970s, and my dad is called Clement, after some bloke who ran Studio One Records in Jamaica, according to Gramps. In fact only Gramps and my mum have names that aren't linked to some Jamaican music person or other. Mum's name is Pearl and Gramps is called Ernest Theophilus Beresford Chambers. Or at least that's what it says on his passport. He's just Gramps at home.

My mum works at the city council. She's high up in some department or other. I don't have a clue what she actually does. She tried to tell me one time and it was so boring that I ended up watching some antiques programme on the TV for fun. It was *that* boring. My dad's got a cool job though. He owns a bar restaurant place in town and doesn't usually get up until after ten in the morning. Whenever my form teacher, Mrs Dooher, tells me off for being late I tell her that it runs in the family. Being late won't stop me from being great, I tell her. Seen? Only she never has a clue what I'm saying half the time. Still, she is like fifty or something. Lovely with it though.

Every morning since I met his raggedy ass at primary school, I call for my best mate, Jit. He lives down a side street off Evington Road, almost opposite the one my family live on and most times he'll be waiting outside his front door for me. He won't walk down to the main road to make things easier. And he doesn't wait in his front room for me to get there before coming out, which is what I would do. Nah, he just stands there, on the pavement, looking like the nutter that he is. This morning though he wasn't there and I thought that he was bunking off school again. He does that sometimes, a couple of days here and there when no one sees him and he don't pick up the phone. I don't know why and he never tells me, but then again I don't really ask. That 'let's talk about everything' stuff is for girls, anyway. My man will tell me when him good and ready.

I walked up to his front door, which needed a serious lick of paint, and knocked. The bell stopped working a couple of years ago and his mum, who he lives with, has never had it fixed. His dad lives on the other side of town and he never sees Jit. Something to do with family honour and stuff that I don't get. I call it the 'Asian ting' whenever it comes up which is like once a year maybe. I'm sure he'll tell me about it properly, one of these days. I waited for Jit to answer and gave him a minute, tops. Usually if he hasn't answered by then, I'm gone. In sixty seconds, like in that lame film. I'd counted to twenty-five when he answered, looking all shady like Slim.

'Easy Dean,' he said, opening the door.

'*Yes, my dan*! An' isn't it a lovely *bright* mornin' too?' I replied, mimicking our headmaster, Mr Black.

Jit just shrugged at me and edged out of the gap in the

door, like opening it fully would have set off an explosion or something.

'You have dead bodies hidden in there?' I asked as a joke.

'I could hide your dead body . . .' he told me, not even smiling. Weirdo.

We set off on our twenty minute walk to the *wrong* side of town, to go and wait for the bus. We always caught the same one, down by our friend Grace's house, even though we could get one nearer on Evington Road to take us to school. I don't even *remember* why we started doing it, but it's like a tradition now and I wouldn't feel right if we didn't walk all that way. By the time we reached the stop though, Grace was already gone, or so we thought, and we had to amuse ourselves by taking the piss out of a couple of lads from school, Robert Sargeant and Wesley Magoogan. They were talking about some new fantasy book and I *had* to join in.

'. . . of course Gerafaggan is the *evil* one, the dark lord,' Robert was saying.

I looked at Jit and grinned.

'What kind of *name* is that, man?' I asked.

Robert and Wesley looked at me like I was missing my head.

'But he's a character from *The Dark Lord of Hazelwitch*,' replied Wesley, like I was supposed to know what that was. They could have been making it up for all I cared.

'It's really very *good*,' added Robert.

'Yeah but has it got talking animals and that?' I asked.

'Erm . . . yes, I believe it has,' Robert told me.

'There's a giant rat called Tar too – that's *rat* spelt backwards by the way,' said Wesley, getting really excited.

'Hey, Fartyfartkins the Smelly or whatever yer name is – I look *stupid* to you?' I replied. Like, is *tar* really *rat* spelt *backwards*?

Wesley looked down at his feet.

'Any fit women in it?' asked Jit.

'I think that rather depends on your imagination,' Robert told him. 'Of course in one's head a character takes on the features that one would *like* to give them.'

Jit just scratched his head and looked puzzled.

'He means that you can make the woman look like who you want, man,' I explained.

'I *knew* that,' lied Jit.

'In my head,' began Wesley, 'Princess Wondlebarn is actually rather similar to Cat Deeley.'

'Yes, and in my head there's a little hammer striking against the nerves, telling me that this conversation has reached its *nadir*,' I replied.

Wesley and Robert looked at each other and carried on their discussion. Jit shook his head.

'Man, I bet that's all you do – look up shit in a dictionary all night . . .'

'Least I can read,' I said.

'What's it mean, anyway?' he asked, as a familiar estate car pulled up alongside the bus stop and Grace smiled at us.

'It means like the end. The lowest point of any particular thing . . .'

'I swear you're turning into one of *them*, bro,' Jit said to me, as we opened the car door and got in. He didn't tell me who '*them*' were though.

Grace turned round and gave us a big smile.

'My two favourite smelly pants . . .' she said.

'Easy, Sister Gee,' I replied.

'Yeah . . . er . . . hello,' added Jit, giving Grace this funny look. It's a look he often gives her and I think it means that he likes her but he isn't sure how to make it obvious. But he doesn't need to anyway. Everyone except him and Grace know that they fancy each other. Man should just ask her out, I reckon.

Her dad turned and smiled too.

'Hello lads – how are we this morning. *Kickin'* or *stink*, as you young 'uns like to say?'

'*Dad*!' said Grace, getting embarrassed, like she always does when her dad tries to pretend he's in with the kids.

'We're cool, Mr Parkhurst,' I replied.

'Yeah, we's *kickin'*, man,' agreed Jit.

'Excellent – and call me Michael, please . . .'

He pushed a CD into the stereo and a load of trumpet nonsense blasted out of the speakers.

'Miles Davis,' he told us as we drove off.

'Got his *every* CD,' I muttered, having a laugh, even though I actually quite liked it. Not that I was going to tell Grace's dad.

TWO

Mr Black was waiting at the school gates as Grace's dad parked up and let us out. Normally Black would have told us off for being late but we were only a couple of minutes out and he just smiled at us before talking to Grace's dad for a bit.

'Good morning, Michael!' he boomed in his deep voice as we made our way into school.

'Your dad and Black are like best mates,' Jit told Grace.

'No they're not,' replied Grace, looking all sheepish.

'Best thing, I reckon,' I told them.

'Why is that, then?' asked Jit.

'It's like he's on our side and that,' I told him. 'We get into trouble and Mr Parkhurst can help us out – like he did with them lunch time clubs.'

I was talking about a scam that had backfired a few weeks earlier. I had convinced my friends that we should join these boring social clubs that run at lunchtime, just so that we wouldn't have to have late lunches. Only we went a bit far and got into trouble. Grace's dad saved us though.

'He won't do that all the time,' said Grace.

'Would if *you* asked him,' I told her.

'Why would I do that, smelly pants?' she replied.

"Cause you love us,' I said.

Jit gave me a funny look, like I was trying it on or something. I just shook my head at him.

'Don't get your panties in a—' I began.

'GET TO YOUR FORM ROOMS!' boomed another familiar voice. It was Mr Herbert, one of the English teachers and Enemy No. 1.

'That's what we're doin',' replied Jit.

'Not fast enough,' snapped Herbert.

'You want us to run?' I asked him.

'Run and fall *over* and break a bone or two?' added Grace. 'Then we'd *have* to go to hospital and the doctors would ask us what happened and *we'd* say that *you* told us to run and then my dad would *have* to sue the school and it would all just end up in a *terrible* mess . . .'

'Shut it, Grace and get going or I'll add you to my detention list,' warned Herbert.

Jit looked at me, mouthed a swear word and then mumbled under his breath.

'Like we care, you *knob* . . .'

'I BEG YOUR PARDON?'

Herbert's face was all red. Loads of the other kids at school would have pooped it but Jit just grinned.

'Nuttin', sir,' he said. 'Can you stop talking though – I mean how are we supposed to get to registration if you keep us here in the corridor?'

'Just get going,' Herbert told us through gritted teeth.

'Later,' said Jit, as we walked down towards our form room.

Mrs Dooher was waiting for us as we arrived and I pulled up a chair next to Imtiaz and Hannah, two more of my friends. Jit couldn't find a seat so he stood where he was, like he was lost.

'Grab a seat, Jit,' said Mrs Dooher in her soft Liverpool accent.

'I'm OK standing, Miss,' he said.

'You can always sit on my knee,' said Suky, the other friend in our little gang of six.

'Or mine,' added Grace.

'He'd *love* that,' grinned Hannah.

As the class started to giggle, Jit didn't move and looked to me for help. I budged up and he came across and shared my seat with me.

'We need more chairs, Miss!' shouted a lad called Dilip.

'Yes – we do,' agreed Mrs Dooher. 'It's just a shame that so many get broken by you lot . . .'

'Ain't our fault,' said Dilip's mate, Mohammed.

'It *isn't* our fault, Mohammed,' corrected Mrs Dooher.

'Yeah, but . . .'

Mrs Dooher ignored him.

'Right – there are a lot of notices to get through so listen up, class. And can someone take charge of collecting entries for the school quiz. I need four of you to enter . . .'

As she went through the notices, I opened my bag to show Jit the CDs. I sold loads of stuff at school to make a bit of pocket money. It was easy to do. My brother always had things to sell, and often I'd take the money and give Jit some of it. Most of the time he helped to flog the stuff anyway. 'How much?' he whispered.

'Gussie said a fiver but I reckon sevens, man. That way he gets *four* quid and we get a quid-fifty each,' I whispered back.

'Cool . . .' replied Jit.

'Anything you'd like to share with us, Dean?' asked Mrs Dooher.

'Nah, nuttin' Miss,' I replied.

'What about five million pounds – you'd love to share that . . . !' shouted Dilip.

'If I had five million pounds why would I want to share it wit' your ugly ass?' I asked. The divv.

'OK lads! That's enough. Get to your lessons,' said Miss.

The room filled with the sound of chairs scraping on

the floor and the rustle of bags and coats. I winked at Jit and told him we'd go over the stuff at break.

'Go over what?' asked Grace.

'Mind your own, Sister Gee,' I told her.

'You sellin' porno mags again?' asked Hannah.

'That's disgusting,' said Suky.

'Stinky perverts . . .' added Grace, jokingly.

I didn't say anything straight away. Instead I counted to ten, waiting for Imtiaz to say something that he thought was mature. Something to back up Suky. I got to three.

'. . . yeah – that's terrible,' he said, looking at the girls.

'Like you ain't never seen a dirty mag,' said Jit, wading in on my side as usual.

'I don't look at them at all,' replied Imtiaz, acting all big and clever.

'Nah – you is too busy on the Internet sites to do that,' I said, laughing. 'That time when me and Jit came over to your house – you remember . . . ?' I turned to the girls. '. . . he showed us this site where there were pictures of Angelina Jolie and—'

'Shut up, Dean,' said Imtiaz, quickly.

'We don't want to know anyway,' Hannah told us both.

'Don't worry – it's not your fault,' Suky said to me. 'Your hormones will catch up in a couple of years.'

'Nice one!' grinned Hannah.

I looked at Jit and then at the rest of them. 'Come on, man,' I said to Jit, pretending to be hurt. 'We know when we ain't welcome . . .'

Jit was about to say something but I grabbed him by the arm and pulled him out of the room.

'But what's in the bag?' Grace called out behind us.

'No! You called us *perverts* . . .' I shouted back.

'Stinky bum . . . !' I heard her reply as me and Jit joined the surge of kids heading for the first lesson. It was like falling into a fast flowing river.

At break me and Jit went and hid in one of the cubicles in the toilets and locked the door. I opened my bag and got out a handful of CDs. Jit looked through them.

'It's mostly chart stuff,' he said, not impressed.

'Yeah, but that's what they's all listenin' to,' I reminded him.

'Ain't you got no hip hop or anything?'

I shook my head at him, as I heard someone come into the toilets and lowered my voice.

'It's about making dough, man. Not what we want to hear but what we can sell . . .'

'Yeah but . . .'

Someone approached the door to the cubicle and I put a finger to my lips. As I waited for the person to go away, I saw some graffiti on the wall. Someone had tried to wipe it away but hadn't finished the job and I could still make out the words to a rap that I had written about Herbert. I smiled at Jit and pointed at the wall. Jit shrugged. Whoever was listening walked out and we opened the door.

'I'll start asking around,' said Jit.

'Yeah – seven quid each, remember.'

'Cheaper than Asda,' replied Jit, walking out of the toilets. I followed him.

Out in the corridor I spotted a lad called Jason Patel. He was a bully and he hated me and Jit. I tried not to catch his eye but didn't manage it.

'What you lookin' at?' he asked, as the two lads he was with started to grin.

'Nuttin',' I told him, going to walk off.

Jason grabbed my arm and squeezed it.

'Best not be either . . .' he warned. 'Look at me like that again and I'll kick your head in.'

From nowhere Jit appeared and shoved Jason in the chest. 'Move, man!' he shouted.

Everyone in the corridor stopped to stare. I looked at Jit and hoped that he would get the look on my face and leave it alone. But Jit gets a bit funny about stuff and I could tell that he was in one of his moods.

'You stupid?' asked Jason.

'Leave him alone,' said Jit.

Jason let go of my arm and squared up to Jit. He was at least five inches taller than my mate and he was hard as nails. Everyone in school avoided him if they could. Not Jit though. Just as I was about to calm the whole thing down and say sorry, Jason slapped Jit and then head-butted him. I felt my whole body go tense and my stomach fell. Jit just stood there though, his eyes watering. There was blood around his nose.

'You want some more?' asked Jason, standing back, holding his hands in fists.

'If you like,' replied Jit, in a whisper.

'You're mad, man,' grinned Jason. 'You must like gettin' beat up.'

Jit looked at Jason. His eyes were wild.

'My mum hits me harder than that,' he told Jason.

Jason grabbed his hair and punched him a few more times. I jumped in and tried to stop it but Jason's friends pushed me out of the way. When Jason let Jit go there was blood all down his top and he was crying.

'You don't never leave it, do you?' spat Jason, before walking off quickly with his mates, disappearing outside just as Mr Singh, our football coach arrived with Miss Khan, who taught English.

'What's happened here?' asked Singh.

Someone shouted that Jit had been beaten up.

'Is that what happened, Jit?' asked Singh.

Jit wiped his eyes but didn't say a word.

'Who saw Jit getting beaten up?' Miss Khan asked the crowd, only no one replied because they were too scared of Jason Patel to snitch on him.

I began to say something but Jit glared at me and I shut up.

'It was nuttin', sir,' he told Singh. 'I bumped into the door . . .'

Singh looked at Jit and shook his head.

'Come on,' he said to him. 'Let's get you to the medical room.'

I started to follow but Singh told me to say where I was.

'I think I need to have a little chat with Jit on my own,' he said to me.

I shrugged and watched Jit being led away, as Grace and Hannah walked up, looking all worried.

'What happened?' asked Hannah.

I shrugged again.

'I dunno – we was just walking out of the loo and Jason grabbed me and that. Then he beat up Jit . . .'

Grace's face fell and tears welled up in her eyes.

'Is he all right?' she asked.

'Dunno – Singhy took him to the medical room,' I replied.

'Did he grass on Jason?' asked Hannah.

'Nah – he'll just get beat up again if he does . . .'

Grace told us that she was going to see if Jit was OK and Hannah said that someone should grass Jason up. But that wasn't going to happen and Hannah knew it too. Jason would just wait for me in the street if I told on him and there'd be no one to jump in and stop it. I picked up my bag and walked off to our next lesson, still in shock at what had happened. It was out of nothing too, like being hit by lightning or something. But our school is like that sometimes.

THREE

I didn't see Jit again for the rest of the day and when I went round to his house in the evening, the curtains were drawn. No one answered the door when I knocked so I went home and played CDs all night. The ones that I was supposed to sell at school for Gussie. They were rubbish, most of them, but every now and then I found a tune worth listening to. Gussie came into my room around half past ten and asked me if I'd made any money. I told him that I was going to get on with it the following day.

'Seen yer mate, Jit, earlier,' he said.

'Where?' I asked.

'Down Evington Road – with his face all mash-up. He hit a parked bus or summat?'

'Nah – just some fight he got into at school . . .'

I played with the idea of telling Gussie all about Jason Patel and his bullying, but in the end I didn't say anything. Gussie would have sorted Jason out too, but then the whole school would know that I was scared of Jason and called in my older brother to fight for me.

That was a rep I could do without. Instead I watched TV until I fell asleep.

The next morning I called for Jit as usual but got no reply. All the curtains were drawn and I couldn't hear a sound. I waited for about five minutes and knocked as hard as I could but it didn't help. I decided that Jit was taking the day off and walked down towards Grace's house. But when I got to the bus stop Grace didn't turn up either and I had to ride to school with Robert and Wesley sitting behind me, talking about the latest chapter of that book. The one that I thought they had made up. I didn't get involved this time though. Instead I started making up a rhyme in my head about Jit. I didn't get very far before I got bored and in the end I just sat and watched the world go by until it was time to get off.

As I got into my form room though, Jit was already there, laughing about something with Grace. His face was swollen round one eye and his nose was twice its normal size. I walked over and pulled up a chair by Hannah, who Jit and me had known since we were little.

'Hey Dean,' she said, smiling like she was mad.

'Sister Aitch.'

'You look lost. What's up?'

I shrugged.

'Nuttin',' I replied.

'Must be something because your face looks like it's been slapped hard by a big man with rings on,' she told me.

'I just been on a wild goose chase – that's all. First I called for Jit and then I waited for Sister Gee but they didn't show. And then I get to school and here they are . . . *early.*'

'Yeah, I thought that was a bit weird. They were here before me and that's *never* happened before.'

Jit looked over at me just then and I nodded to him, all cool and that. He raised an eyebrow and then got out of his seat and walked over.

'Yes, D!' he said smiling.

'Easy . . .'

'Whassup, man?'

'Where was you this mornin'? I called for you and then I walked down to the stop . . .' I told him.

'Yeah – sorry 'bout that. I went round to Grace's house early and we got a lift in from her dad . . .' he replied, watching my face.

'What – and you never even waited for me?'

Straight after I said it I realised that it made me sound like whining little kid and I wished that I hadn't opened my mouth.

'I was well early, man. I couldn't sleep and then I had to just get out the house – my mum was stressin' me . . .'

'Oh.'

'She's been playin' up and that . . . and I'm gettin' the flak . . .' he began to explain but then something in his eyes changed and he grinned a big wide smile and changed the subject.

'You see that Misha in Year Ten – the one with the green eyes? Rude . . .' he said.

I laughed, and thought about asking him some more about his mum but then I realised that it was his business and he would tell me when he was good and ready. Instead I let it go and grinned.

'Rude ain't the word my dan . . .' I said, before singing a little rhyme that I copied from a ragga DJ called Buju Banton.

'*She haffe walk like a champion, talk like a champion,*
What a piece a' body gal, tell me weh yuh get it from . . .'

I was just about to get to the rudest bit when Mrs Dooher walked in and told me be quiet.

'But *Miss*,' I complained. 'I was about to get to the good bit, man.'

'Save it for the playground,' Mrs Dooher replied, shuffling through a load of papers.

Grace smiled at me.

'What's the next bit?' she said.

'Too dutty fe you, Sister Gee. I don't want no one talkin' 'bout how I corrupted no little innocent gal . . .'

'I *hate* you,' joked Grace.

'Not that you even know what he was on about,' added Hannah.

'*Yeah*,' joined in Jit.

'Anyway, my brother used to play that tune and it's dirty,' continued Hannah. 'Seriously, Grace, you're better off not knowing what comes next . . .'

'*Oh*! You horrible people!' said Grace, like a three-year-old who didn't get an ice cream.

'Grace!'

'Sorry Miss,' she said, going red.

I whispered to her, 'I'll tell you when you're a woman.'

Grace gave me a strange look and then she stuck her fingers up at me. I stuck my tongue out and then listened as Mrs Dooher told us a load of uninteresting things about school.

At lunchtime I sat with my friends in one of the computer rooms and pretended that I was interested in the school magazine that we had to put together. Hannah, Imi and Suky had taken it over from day one and they acted like it was theirs. Every now and again I said something to wind them up – like Imi would ask if anyone had any ideas for a feature story and I'd suggest the mating rituals of cockroaches or something – but mostly I just let them get on with it. I didn't mind. I spent the time chatting to

Jit or thinking up rhymes. But during that particular lunchtime I had other things on my mind. Jit was trying to play Mine Sweeper on a computer as I spoke to him. Only he didn't get the rules and was getting angry with it.

'Stupid game!' he said for about the tenth time.

'Leave that man,' I said to him. 'Let's go and flog some of these CDs.'

'We's supposed to be workin' on the school paper,' he reminded me.

I thought about it for a moment. 'Let's go and do some research, innit? Out there in the wild corridors of Devana High. Gotta keep in touch with the readers and that . . .' I replied, winking.

'The wannabe adults ain't gonna go for that,' said Jit, talking about Suky and Imi.

'Jus' lef dat to me, my brother,' I told him.

I turned in my chair and watched as Imi tried to work out a problem with the software that Grace's dad had donated to the school. It was a design thing, one that helped to create newspaper templates and magazines but it may as well have been a Latin book to me.

'*Yo!* Editor *bwoi* . . . me an' Jit are gonna head out and do some research, man,' I shouted.

Imi looked up from the screen and grinned.

'Research? Into what?' he asked. '*Misha* . . . ?'

'Yeah man,' I grinned back, 'we're gonna write about the difference between boys and girls and that . . . *educational*, my dan, you get me?'

'Nah – but then again you talk like an idiot,' said Imi, returning to the screen.

'Kiss my fat ass. *Twice*,' I told him, getting up.

'So can we expect a piece on teenagers and their relationships then?' asked Grace, as Jit joined me.

'That sounds a bit lame to me,' I said. 'You might get a lyrics on summat though.'

'What's a "lyrics" mean, Dean?' asked Grace.

'Just what you did there, Sister Gee. A rhyme, man. You know if poetry was called *lyrics*, I reckon more of the yout' would go for it . . .' I told her.

'Like them poetry slams at the community centre?' asked Hannah.

'Yeah – you get me . . . ?' I replied.

'*Ehhh*! No thanks,' she said, smiling.

'Dunno what you're *missin'*, Sister Aitch,' I said, jokingly.

'I've seen your bedroom,' grinned Hannah. '*Believe me – I know . . .*'

'Evil woman . . . ! You can kiss my *double* fat ass. *Three times*,' I replied, heading out of the door with Jit.

We walked out to the tennis courts where there were a couple of football games in full swing and stood by the steps. There were groups of kids hanging around and chatting and I unzipped my bag and pulled out a handful of CDs.

'Go for the ones that live near Grace and Suky,' I told Jit.

Our school was a bit of an experiment by the people that ran the education department, or at least that's what my dad once told me. They took half of each year group from round my way, an area which was not exactly known for its money; and half of them from the area where Grace, Imi and Suky lived, which was called posh and where everyone had big houses and lots of money. Thing was, *my* family lived in a big house and we had enough money but that didn't make *us* posh, just because of the area we lived in, which I thought was really funny. Adults are some messed up people, man, with their prejudices and that. Jit eyed up Robert and Wesley who were with a bunch of their friends. As we walked over I realised that they were still discussing the same book.

'. . . Princess Wondlebarn has got the ancient flute of Kings,' Wesley was telling everyone else, as I interrupted him.

'And the great goblin Ganglefart is going to eat her,' I said.

The group of friends looked at me like I was crazy, as Jit stood and grinned. I showed them my goods.

'CDs, man – all the latest stuff. Rock, pop, indie – you wan' it, we got it . . .'

'I don't think you're supposed to sell things at school,' said Robert.

'Who says that?' asked Jit.

'I'm just sure that it's against the rules,' he added.

I looked at Wesley and shrugged.

'Well, if it's *rules* you're goin' to play by – you may as well go to the local shops and spend *thirteen* big quid on them. You don't *want* half price CDs if it's *rules* that you look to . . .'

Wesley looked around his group of friends and then spoke. 'Did you say *half price?*' he asked.

'Nearly,' I replied, holding out the CDs for him. 'I want sevens for 'em. Not a penny less and not six pound more like in the shops . . .'

'But they're all copies,' said Robert, after taking one and studying it like it was a text book.

'That's right – genuine, first generation, burned by my own two hands, copies . . .' I admitted.

'But . . .' began Wesley.

'*Wesley, Wesley, Wesley,*' I said. 'When you're at home downloading tunes from the net without paying – that's the same thing . . .'

'But you can't do that any more,' Robert told me. 'You have to pay now . . .'

'Even better . . . I'm offering you brand new CDs – I've even taken out the chore of copying them – just for you . . .'

Robert looked through the rest of the selection and then smiled. He held up a CD by some punk skater band, all in baggy trousers and with stupid beards.

'Seven pounds, you say.'

'If I'm lyin' I'm flyin', Roberto,' I told him, copying something that I heard in a film once.

'They really are a rather wicked band,' said Robert.

'That's my boy,' I said with a huge grin. 'What's seven quid when you've got the latest offering from a rather wicked band, right there in your hand?'

Robert looked around his group of friends, as though he was waiting for one of them to tell him no. When they didn't speak he pulled out his wallet and handed me a tenner. I had five pound coins in my pocket and gave him his change.

'See? Nuttin' so nice as handin' over yer money when you know that you've got yourself a proper, *one hundred percent*, bargain, man,' I said, as his friends asked to look at the rest of the stash.

'An' remember,' I continued. 'I ain't no supermarket. *Sold as seen*, my likkle fantasy reading bredren . . . you get me?'

Robert gave me a funny look and shrugged.

FOUR

I asked Jit about Jason on the way home. We were walking up Evington Road, past a load of takeaway shops and my stomach was rumbling as the smell of food wafted around the street.

'I ain't gonna do nuttin',' Jit told me. 'What *can* I do?'

'You didn't have to get involved,' I told him.

'What? And leave my best mate to get picked on – I'd rather get beaten up,' replied Jit.

I was going to say something, but the way Jit had said what he did made me feel proud to have him as my friend and I told him that I would talk to Gussie for him.

'Straighten it out. If you like . . .' I said to him.

Jit shrugged. 'Ain't worth it. If Gussie batters Jason then we'll just get more shit from him at school. And what about when we're out . . . nah, best just leave it. He'll get his, man. He's not gonna be bigger than us for the rest of his life, is he?'

'I don't even know why he picks on us,' I said. 'I mean it ain't like we ask for it . . .'

Jit grinned. 'Apart from the last time, when I shoved him . . .' he said.

'Yeah well – thanks for that, man. You saved me there.'

We crossed a side street and walked past a grocer's. There was an old man, a local homeless bloke, standing outside the shop. He had grey hair that was matted into dirty dreadlocks and he stank. As the people entering and leaving the shop tried to ignore him, he held out a wooden stick like it was a sword and pretended to fight someone.

'. . . Mash yuh up!' he was shouting at no one.

We ignored him, walking past quickly so that he wouldn't try to talk to us like he normally did. We called him MC Nutty although I had no idea what his real name was.

'How much we make on the CDs?' Jit asked me.

'Give me a moment and I'll do you a profit and loss sheet,' I said.

I stopped and opened my bag, counting the CDs. There had been thirty in there in the morning and now there were nineteen. Not bad for one day.

'We sold eleven – that's seventy-seven quid,' I told him.

Jit's eyes nearly popped out of his head.

'That's some good dough,' he said.

'Still gotta give Gussie his money out of that,' I reminded him.

'So what's that make then?' he asked.

'Four quid a CD – work it out.'

We walked on, both of us quiet as our brains tried to do the maths. It was like a contest to see who would come up with the figures first and I was confident that I'd win. Too confident though.

'Forty-eight quid to him,' I said.

'Nah,' said Jit, correcting me. 'Eleven fours is forty-four man. That leaves us thirty-three.'

I looked at him in amazement. Jit hated maths and never paid attention in school. Maybe I'd found another way to teach him, I thought, as I dreamt up my own teach yourself maths text book, one that would make me loads of money.

'. . . So that's sixteen-fifty each,' he concluded.

'Yeah – I'll double-check it at home but I think you're right,' I said.

Jit stopped at the end of his street and looked at me.

'Any chance you can let me have a fiver, man?' he asked.

'Yeah – later. I'll bring it round,' I replied, not getting what he meant.

'I meant now, bro,' he said, looking embarrassed.

'Oh – right . . . yeah, no worries,' I said.

Jit waited for a moment before explaining. 'It's just that my mum is workin' late and she ain't left me no dinner,' he said.

'That's cool, man. You don't have to explain,' I told him.

'So I need some dough to get some chips or summat . . .' he continued. 'And I ain't got no bus fare for the mornin' . . .'

And then he just stopped, like he'd realised what he'd said and didn't like it. I pulled out some money and gave it to him. It was a tenner.

'There you go, brother,' I said. 'Although you could always come eat round at mine . . . Mum would love it. She's always complaining that I don't bring me mates home.'

'Maybe another night,' said Jit, pocketing the money. 'I'll check you tomorrow.'

'I was gonna bring the rest round later,' I said to him.

'I gotta do some shit for me mum,' said Jit, as he turned to leave.

I was going to say something but I left it and watched him walk off up the street. I knew that something was up with him but I didn't want to be all girlie and ask him about it. I knew that he'd tell me soon enough. Instead I headed home and wondered whether I should have charged eight pounds for the CDs instead of seven.

Gussie was waiting for me when I got in and asked for his money before I'd had a chance to sit down.

'Hol' yer horses, bro, I ain't even got me jacket off yet,' I protested.

'Just hand me my money Dean and stop with yer nonsense.'

'Let me sort out my stuff first,' I said, not wanting Gussie to see that I had more money than I was supposed to have.

I took off my jacket and headed up two flights of stairs to my room, locking the door when I got in. I counted out the money quickly, hiding the rest of mine and Jit's and then I took Gussie's cut downstairs.

'Cool,' he said, as he counted it. 'Them things goin' like hot cakes, man.'

'Yeah,' I said in agreement. 'Should get rid of the rest by the end of the week. You gettin' any more?'

'Yeah, man – as many as you need. Got something even better for you soon,' he told me.

I looked at him and raised an eyebrow.

'What?' I asked.

'Mobiles, man. Nuff of dem . . .'

I found the remote for the telly and turned it on, sitting down, but ignoring the screen. 'How much?' I asked him.

'Dunno yet,' Gussie told me. 'My mate, Raj, is getting them. Top of the range ones too.'

'Raj owns that phone shop on East Park Road don't he?'

'*Yeah* – so what?' asked my brother.

'So why can't he sell them there?' I said to him.

It made perfect sense to me. What was the point in having the shop if you gave other people phones to sell?

'Extra stock – off the books and that, you get me?' Gussie said. 'My man needs to get rid so I'm buying the excess . . .'

'Still don't get it,' I admitted.

'All *you* need to get is the dough for the phones, man. You'll make a *load* on them,' promised Gussie.

I was about to say something else but I stopped when I realised that he was right. I wouldn't be making small change out of them. But then again, I thought, would anyone at school have the money to buy phones in the first place? I thought about that as Gussie stood up and told me he was off to see a mate.

'You comin' back for dinner?'

'Nah – tell Mum I'll get summat in town,' he said. 'I gotta do a shift with Dad at eight, anyways . . .'

'Good,' I said. 'Means more food for me, Mr Rotund.'

'You what?' he said, looking puzzled.

'Nuttin' man. Get a dictionary,' I replied.

'What – and end up like you? No thanks, man.'

He walked out of the house and left me to think about who I'd try to sell the mobiles to. My Gramps walked in as I was thinking and farted real loud. It sounded like he had thunder in his pants and the smell was like something that had died with the dinosaurs.

'*Gramps!*' I said, laughing. 'Tha's nasty, man.'

'A nuh nuttin'. Betta fe get it out than keep it in . . .' he replied, sitting down and watching the telly with me, with not even a second thought to the nuclear fart he had just ripped.

After I'd eaten my dinner I walked to Grace's house. She had called to say that her and Hannah were in her basement, going over stuff for the school paper. I told her that I'd come over but when she asked me to call for Jit on the way, I told her that he was busy.

'Oh right,' she'd replied, sounding disappointed.

'What – I'm not good enough on my own?' I teased.

'Yeah!' she said quickly. 'I just hoped that Jit would come round too.'

'You'll have to forget about snogging him for one night,' I told her.

'Stinky git,' she said.

When I got to her house, her mum let me in and asked me how I was.

'Haven't seen you for a few days,' she said.

'I've been busy, Mrs Parkhurst,' I said, in my best accent, trying to impress.

'Homework?' she asked, smiling at me.

'Yes – and other stuff, er . . . things,' I replied.

'Well I'd better let you get downstairs what with the deadline for the paper looming . . .'

'OK.'

I headed down the stairs, hearing a White Stripes CD playing.

'Elvis is in da building!' I said as I walked in.

'Greetings Elvis – tell me, does Heaven have reality TV?' asked Hannah.

'Eh?'

'Reality TV . . .' she repeated.

'What about it, you loony tunes?' I said.

'Cause if it does, do the losers have to go to Hell?'

I just looked at her and shook my head. 'You need to get out more, Sister Aitch. Thirteen and with a head full of shite already . . .'

'Oh *hello* Grace – thanks for inviting me *round* – think I'll *ignore* you though and pretend like you're not even here . . .' said Grace.

'Easy Sister Gee – didn't see you there,' I joked.

'There'll be trouble, my lad,' she said, imitating Mr Black.

'Oh, be firm with me,' I begged. 'Firm but fair . . . !'

'Will you both shut up,' said Hannah.

I stuck my tongue out at her and went and racked up the balls on Grace's snooker table, ready to play a game.

'Who's first for a beatin'?' I asked.

'We asked you round to help us sort out the paper,' said Grace.

'What's wrong with Imi and Suky?' I asked. 'They're the *editors* . . .'

'Imi's at some family do and Suky has got some homework to do,' replied Hannah.

'So you sent for the substitute?' I asked.

'No – you're supposed to be helping us too,' said Grace.

Hannah shook her head and got up from her seat. She walked over to me and grabbed the pool cue from my hand.

'From what I remember, Dean, it's your fault that we have to do this anyway,' she said, menacingly.

'Easy, sister . . . no need to get violent,' I said with a grin.

Hannah poked me in the chest and then cracked into a smile.

'I tell you what – it's only because I've known you since you were a snotty nosed three-year-old that I don't stick that cue right up your ar—'

'Anyone like a drink?' Grace's dad interrupted from the foot of the stairs.

Hannah went bright red.

'Can I have juice please, Dad,' said Grace.

'Yeah, me too,' I said. 'Please.'

'And what about you Hannah? Once you've finished putting that cue where the sun doesn't shine,' grinned Mr Parkhurst.

'Can I have a coffee . . . ?' asked Hannah, grinning back.

Grace's dad suddenly got all excited.

'Ah coffee! Good choice, Hannah, only I've just this morning acquired—' he began.

'You're for it now,' said Grace. 'He got a new toy this morning – a coffee machine – and now he's going to bore us all silly with how it works and we'll never get this work done.'

I thought about the coffee machine at my dad's bar. 'Has it got one of them steam thingys,' I asked.

'Sure has . . .' said Mr Parkhurst.

'Cool!' said Hannah.

'I'll show you how it works if you like,' said Mr Parkhurst.

Grace let out a moan and then started calling everything she could see, the pens, the paper, the snooker table, *everything*, stinky bums.

FIVE

Soon everyone in our year knew about the CDs and Jit and me managed to shift the lot in two days. I even got a few more off Gussie on demand – they were going faster than bullets. By the Thursday evening of that week, me and Jit were sitting in the computer room, counting our money and waiting for the school day to end so that we could play for Devana High in a school league match. It was against one of our most hated rivals, a school from the other side of the city, and we were really up for it. The last time we had played against them, it had been at their school and we'd been racially abused throughout the game by their supporters. Now it was our turn to get some revenge. Imi, who captained the team, kept on giving us little pep talks to get us going and even Mr Singh was excited. The whole year knew about it and we were going to get loads of supporters to watch the game.

'Can't wait,' said Jit, pocketing his money after counting it again.

'This time we're gonna stuff 'em,' I said, remembering

how they had won a penalty in the final minute of the last game to equalise.

'Yeah – this time the ref's gonna be our coach . . .'

Mr Singh would be running the match, just as the other team's coach did at their place, so we were sure that they wouldn't get a dodgy decision go their way. Their coach had been crap – ignoring all the abuse and telling us to get on with the game, like it was OK to get called those names. I'd had to bite my lip throughout the game, something that I don't like doing but when Mr Singh had lodged an official complaint, nothing was done about it. It was pure Babylon, as my dad had said, when I told him.

'They ain't gonna talk no shit either,' I said. 'Not with our fans there this time.' I turned to the girls. 'You lot comin' to watch us later?' I asked.

'*Yeah*!' replied Grace and Hannah together.

'Cool,' I said, waiting for the cheeky remark. It was Grace who made it.

'We couldn't *possibly* miss the opportunity to watch you three in your *little* shorts . . .'

'All that lovely man muscle . . .' added Hannah.

'More like *boy* muscle,' corrected Grace.

'Like twiglets with bottoms attached to them, even . . .'

I shook my head at them. 'Girls, girls . . . what you gonna *do*. You is *too* embarrassed to tell us that you think we is *fine* so haffe mek joke to cover it up . . . it's *sad*, man.'

'You saying I've got skinny legs?' asked Jit, suddenly waking up to the fact that there was a conversation going on.

'Er . . . *yeah*. Have you looked in a *mirror* recently . . . ?' said Hannah.

Jit looked at me.

'Don't be askin' me, bro – I don't never look 'pon your legs no-how,' I said.

'A good thing too . . .' said Jit.

'I think you've got *nice* legs, Jit,' said Grace.

Jit looked at me again and I shrugged.

'Er . . . yeah . . . look we gonna do this paper or what?' he said, changing the subject.

Hannah winked at Grace and then grinned at me. 'See how the bwoi a change subject,' she teased.

'Shut up, Hannah,' said Jit, glaring at her.

'It's OK if you fancy Grace – you only have to say so . . .'

'Oh *piss* off!' replied Jit.

I could see that he was getting wound up so I gave Grace a nudge and she jumped in.

'Leave Jit alone, Hannah-Banana,' she said.

'I was only playin',' replied Hannah.

'I *suggest*,' boomed a voice from the door, 'that you *play* a little less and *work* a little more . . .'

We turned to see Mr Black and Mrs Leecross, our maths teacher, at the door.

'Sorry sir . . .' said Grace. 'We're just getting it done now . . .'

'Good, good,' said Black.

'Anything interesting in it?' asked Leecross.

'No fractions – if that's what you mean,' replied Jit.

Mrs Leecross smiled. 'I could set you some if you like,' she answered.

'We're only short of one feature,' said Hannah quickly, before Jit got the chance to get himself into trouble with his big mouth.

'So are we missing the deadline?' asked Black. 'Only I've told everyone that it will be ready next week and I can't be made to look silly.'

'Oh, no, sir,' said Grace. 'We'll get something in . . .'

'What about a bit of poetry?' asked Black.

'What a splendid idea,' beamed Leecross.

The others looked at me.

'Er . . . could it be like modern stuff,' I asked.

'Well I've been re-reading William Blake recently so I was hoping for something traditional – maybe a piece on Blake's life and a few of his poems . . .'

'Oh . . .' I said, trying not to sound disappointed but failing.

'What do you have in mind, Mr Chambers?' asked Black.

'Well I was gonna write something that was about the school – and maybe write about how Rap is like modern poetry . . .'

'Rap . . . ?' began Mrs Leecross frowning.

'Oh yes, Nancy,' said Black, using Leecross's first name by mistake. 'I've been reading a lot of articles recently about youth culture and the rise of urban poetry . . .'

Mrs Leecross went slightly red and looked away but Black didn't even notice.

'Maybe we could cover the poetry slam at the community centre near us,' added Hannah. 'There's one on Saturday . . .'

'Splendid idea!' he boomed. 'You can cover that, and Dean, I'd like you to do an original piece too, in the *urban* style . . .'

'OK,' I agreed.

'Now get on with it and mind you're good and fit for this evening lads – I've a steak dinner riding on you lot winning . . .' he grinned.

With that he marched out of the room and Leecross followed.

'He's nuts,' said Hannah.

'Proper looped,' agreed Jit.

'Well at least he's not a complete ogre,' said Grace, defending him.

'Yeah,' I agreed, despite myself. 'How many head teachers you reckon there are that know about Rap *and* want it in *their* school paper?'

Jit looked at me the way a shrink looks at a mental patient.

'Poetry's boring,' said Hannah.

'No it ain't,' I argued. 'Not really – we just get taught old stuff, that's all.'

'*Boring* . . .' yawned Jit, agreeing with Hannah.

'Is what you know man – what about Eminem?'

'He's a *rapper*,' said Hannah.

'I read something that called him an urban poet,' Grace told us.

'*Exactly*,' I replied. 'All them rappers is like poets – they just ain't called poets because they swear and that . . .'

'You're wrong in the head, man,' said Jit.

'So you're saying poetry can be *fun*?' asked Hannah.

'Yeah,' I said, looking at Grace, who winked at me.

'Prove it,' challenged Hannah.

'OK then,' I replied. 'I'm gonna write a lyric about school for the paper . . .'

'Can't wait, man,' said Jit, sarcastically.

'Better get on with it,' Hannah told me. 'We need it by the end of the week.'

* * *

Jason Patel caught up with me as I was walking to my next lesson. He was on his own and as I walked by, trying to ignore him, he grabbed me by the arm.

'I hear you've got CDs to sell,' he said.

'*Did* have,' I replied, trying not to let him see that I was in pain from his grip.

'So why didn't you come to me?' he asked.

I shrugged.

'You got any more?' he said, loosening his grip. I pulled my arm away.

'Nah – sold out.'

He moved his head closer to my face.

'Next time you got shit to sell, you let me see first, man.'

'Yeah, cool.'

'I mean it. I find out that you're selling stuff and don't tell me, I'm not gonna be happy.'

'OK,' I said, turning to walk away.

'Best remember, too,' he threatened.

I walked into my lesson and sat down next to Grace. There must have been something in my face because she asked me if I was OK. The lesson was just about to start and Mr Woods asked for us all to shut up, so I whispered my reply.

'I'm cool, man. Just bumped into a snake in the corridor, that's all.'

The rest of the afternoon dragged by slowly and by the time school finished I had forgotten about what Jason had said. I was too wound up about the football and couldn't wait for it to start. I ran down to the changing rooms with Jit and we started talking about the game, and how many goals we were going to score. Imtiaz was waiting for us, already half changed and we started to get ready too. The rest of the team started arriving soon afterwards, and as I sat on the wooden bench, with my boots next to me, I watched Mr Singh bring in an orange net bag, full of footballs.

'On me head, Singhy!' I shouted.

Mr Singh grinned at me.

'The other school are going to be about half an hour yet so I want you to get out there and get warmed up. Remember I want the stretches done properly *before* you start kicking the balls around.'

'Yeah, yeah,' I said. 'Just pass me a football, sir.'

Mr Singh took a ball out of the net and threw it to me. I grabbed hold of it in one hand, picked up my boots with the other, and headed outside, with Jit and Imtiaz following, just as the sharp smell of Deep Heat started to make my eyes water.

SIX

It felt like half of our year had turned out to support us when we got to the pitch. I looked around for the girls and saw them standing by the halfway line. I walked over, booting the ball up into the air and then chasing after it. It bounced around the centre circle and I misjudged, running straight underneath it. Jit controlled it behind me and started to do keep-ups, which he was really good at. Then he passed the ball to Imi who trapped it, and pushed it on to me with his other foot. We did this for a few minutes and then started doing stretches. As I bent forward to touch my toes I heard a wolf-whistle from behind me. I straightened up and turned to see Hannah grinning at me.

'Nice bum!' she shouted, before bursting into giggles with Suky and Grace. I stuck two fingers up at them and went back to my warm up.

One by one, the rest of the team started to turn up on the pitch. They all started their warm up routines but I'd already finished mine so I got the ball and kicked it towards one of the goals. It ran along the ground into the net and got stuck. I ran over and pulled it free, turning to see Jit and Imi by the penalty spot.

'You go in goal for a minute,' said Imi, as I threw the ball to him. He placed it on the penalty spot and took five steps backwards. Then he ran slowly to the ball and sent it flying past my head, back into the net.

'YEAH!!!' came a shout from the sidelines, as Suky and Hannah jumped up and down.

I threw the ball to Jit and looked for Grace. She was standing with Robert and Wesley, who must have been forced to come along because they never watched football. Robert's face was so red that I could see it from where I stood and I watched as Grace flirted with them both, giggling and playing with her hair. I wondered what she was up to as the ball sailed over my head again.

'GOAAAAL!!!' I heard Jit shout as he did a little jig, copying a Manchester United player, his arms out at his side.

'Only goal you're gonna get,' I said to him. 'You don't ever score in the real games . . .'

'I'm the creator,' he said. 'Weren't for me you'd never get the ball 'cause you don't like tackling . . .'

'What you on about? I'm like Mr Tackling MC, man . . .'

'More like Girlie MC,' said Imi.

'Leave it, posh boy,' I told him. 'You stick to yer books

and yer computer. Dis here's a ghetto bwoi game . . .'

'Shut up, Dean,' said Imi.

'See? You know I'm right.'

I walked away from the goal and took the ball with me, placing it just outside the penalty box, about twenty yards from the goal. Simon, our goalkeeper, jogged to the goal line and turned to face me, as some of the other girls in the crowd started to sing 'Devana, Devana!'

'Top corner, Deano,' said Simon, waiting for me to take my shot.

I concentrated on where I was going to put the ball, and then tried to curl it past the keeper. But I caught the ball wrong and it skidded across the ground and lamely into Simon's hands.

'RUBBISH!' shouted someone from the crowd, as I swore at myself.

Mr Singh blew his whistle and gathered us all together in the centre circle.

'The other team are five minutes away,' he said, 'so you've got fifteen minutes to kill, at least.'

He looked at me and grinned before speaking.

'I suggest that *some* of you use that time to practise your shooting skills,' he said.

Jit and Imi started laughing at me but I ignored them and jogged over to where the girls were standing.

'Deano! Deano!' sang Hannah, before she wolf-whistled again.

'Yes, yes, sisters!' I said, holding my arms out and my palms upwards, like a real poser.

'Nice shorts,' said Suky.

'Must feel real good to know you got a man like me standing talking to you,' I joked.

'Oooh yeah,' said Hannah. 'I'm gonna fall over with excitement in a minute.'

'See me?' I boasted. 'I am the don, the don, the king champion!'

Suky and Hannah burst into laughter.

'See how your head gets bigger every day,' said Suky.

'Hush up and go kiss yer boyfriend,' I told her.

'Who's my boyfriend?' she asked.

'Imi – don't tell me you ain't checking him, man. I *know* . . .'

Suky looked at Hannah.

'*See*?' she said. 'Boys don't know anything . . .'

Grace walked up to us and smiled.

'Hey Brother Dee,' she said, copying *my* joke.

I was about to pull her up on it but Hannah suddenly whispered to us. 'Miss Khan's here,' she said, like that was supposed to be a big time secret or something.

'And?' I asked.

'*Miss Khan? Mr Singh?*' whispered Suky.

'God – don't you know *anything*?' added Grace.

'They're going out with each other,' said Hannah, like the walking Heat magazine that she is.

'How you know that?' I asked.

'It's like, *sooo* obvious,' said Suky, in an American accent.

'Man – you lot are like a bunch of cackling hags,' I said. 'All you do is chat, you know.'

'It's true . . .' said Grace. 'I saw them together in town . . . they were holding *hands*.'

'Big deal, man.'

The girls looked at each other and shook their heads in disgust.

'You just run along back to your little game,' said Hannah.

'*Boys* . . .' added Suky.

'Blabber mout' witches,' I said with a smile, before returning to the other lads.

In our first year at Devana High, Mr Black had managed to get floodlights put in. Our main pitch was used for games all year round, and the local community used it too, the local teams playing on Saturdays and Sundays. By the time that the other school had arrived the lights were just coming on, even though it was still daylight, because by the second half they would be needed. I watched the opposition walk onto the pitch as our supporters booed them and called them names. Not racist ones, like their fans had done to us, just funny ones. The players didn't look around them, they walked on with their heads down, like they were worried. I pointed it out to Imi, who just grinned.

'Let's give them a good reason to be worried,' he said, looking at Jit, who was known for making really hard tackles in the first few minutes of every game, just to see how the other teams reacted.

'I'm ready,' said Jit.

Mr Singh had a quick word with their teacher, who was going to be a linesman, and then signalled to Mr Wilson, who was watching the opposite line. He called Imi and their captain to the centre, spoke to them and then put the ball on the centre spot. They kicked off and passed the ball all the way back to their keeper. I pushed ahead, taking up my position as a forward, coming face to face with one of their biggest players, a lad called Johnno. 'You're getting stuffed this time,' I said to him, watching the ball as it sailed over my head, towards our goal.

'You wish . . .' said Johnno, running to the halfway line with me.

Jit got hold of the ball in midfield and sent it skidding along the ground to the right, where one of our players,

Gary, controlled it, before skipping past their left back and running in towards their goal. Their centre half got in quickly though and made a tackle, winning the ball and sending it back into the middle where I challenged for it with Johnno. He used his elbows to beat me to it and sent me sprawling to the ground, as he headed it away. I got up quickly and glared at him.

'Summat wrong, you monkey?' he said quietly.

'You what?'

'You 'eard me,' he said, chasing after the ball again.

I ran with him, fuming, watched him collect it and then slid in, taking the ball and his legs together. He cried out and swore as Mr Singh blew for a free kick.

'Leave it out, Dean,' Singhy said to me.

'He was callin' me racist names again,' I told him.

Mr Singh looked at me and nodded.

'Well if I hear him – he's going off. You leave the punishment to me,' he said.

The trouble was that Johnno and his team mates were being clever about it. As the game turned into a scrappy mess, they taunted us in whispers, so that Singhy couldn't hear them, and one by one, we got angrier and angrier, even the white lads in our team, who hated the racism as much as we did. By the time the first half was nearly over, I was running around like an angry bull, seeing red. I had one chance which I put over the bar and another that I missed wide, and with about five minutes left I heard Johnno taunting me again.

'This is an English game,' he said. 'You darkies ain't no good at it.'

Jit jogged up beside me as Johnno walked away, laughing to his team mates.

'What did he say?' Jit asked.

'Usual shit,' I replied.

'I'm getting vex, man,' Jit told me.

'Leave it,' I said. 'Let's just beat 'em with the ball . . .'

But Jit, as usual, didn't listen. Gary, Imi and another lad, Matt, created a good opening which their keeper sent out for a corner, and we waited in the box for the delivery. As I was running around, trying to find a space, someone tripped me up and then I heard someone whisper in my face.

'Ever see a flyin' gorilla? Watch the replay . . .'

I looked up and saw a boot connect with my abuser's face. Shouting went up and the two teams got into a scuffle, pushing and shouting and swearing. Gary had Johnno in a head lock and was punching his head and Jit was laying into the lad that had tripped me up. It was like a war zone. When it was all over, Johnno, Gary and Jit were sent off and a few yellow cards were shown to some of the others. I went mad at half time, calling Mr Singh a coward. But he ignored me and said that he wasn't going to tolerate fighting, regardless of the reasons behind it.

The second half went by without any more incidents and right at the end Imi scored from a free kick to win the game but no one was cheering or clapping. Gary and Jit had told everyone watching what had happened and as the opposing team left the pitch some of our fans started to boo them. Then someone threw a drink over their coach and someone else threw a punch, as the crowd surrounded them, mostly the lads but some of the girls too. Mr Singh ran in to try and calm it down, pushing people away but the atmosphere was ugly, like they say in the news, and eventually Mr Black and a few more teachers, who were still at school ran down to the pitch and sorted it all out. Black was going mad, his face all red.

'I'm ashamed of you all!' he was shouting, pushing kids out of the way, yelling at them to go home . . .

SEVEN

'There is a deep sense of shame nestling in my breast this morning, one that I can only attribute to the actions of a small minority of your year, *actions* which took place last night . . .'

The entire year was sitting in the main hall the following morning, listening to Mr Black as he talked about the football. I was right in the middle, sitting next to Hannah and Grace, hoping that he wouldn't pick on Jit or Gary for being sent off. They were both at the back of the hall, Gary with his class, and Jit sitting on his own because he had come in late. When I'd called for him no one answered and he wasn't waiting with Grace when I got to hers either. I don't know where he'd been but I knew it was because he was angry about the game and being red-carded. At least that's what I thought was up with him. Mr Black cleared his throat and continued.

'. . . I'm not *saying* that racism is to be tolerated. It *should* be punished. But not like yesterday. Attacking another school's pupils, *regardless* of what they've done, when they have been invited as *our* guests, is *not* the way of Devana High. It is *not* the civilised response. Now, I know some of you will argue that you were abused and I know that that is *wrong*, but it is up to *us*, as your *teachers*, to sort these problems out. You *don't* do it by jostling and jeering a group of pupils and teachers from another school as though they were elks and you were a pack of wolves . . . oh, some of you *may* snigger but that's what *I* saw last night. Bullying, cowardly actions which I *will not* tolerate. Do I make myself *clear* . . . ?'

'Yessir . . .' replied about half of our year group.

'Right, now get off to your lessons whilst I try and salvage what is left of the goodwill towards our school by telephoning their principal and apologising in person. Good morning, Year Nine . . .'

And with that he stormed out of the hall, closely followed by Herbert and Singh as the kids started to chatter amongst themselves and scrape back their chairs before heading off to first lesson. We had English with Herbert and I walked towards the classroom slowly. Jit was waiting outside the hall for me, and he looked like he had slept in his clothes. There was a strange smell coming from him and his hair was a mess.

'You look like you've been dragged through a hedge, backwards,' I said to him.

He looked right into my eyes and then down at his feet.

'I couldn't sleep,' he told me. 'I was angry about gettin' sent off and then when I did fall asleep, I couldn't get up and I didn't want to be late for school . . .'

'That's a first,' I told him, smiling.

'Didn't even have time to shower,' he said.

'Yeah, I can smell that for myself,' I joked, but then wished that I hadn't opened my big mouth. Jit looked away.

'Only kiddin' bro',' I said, trying to make up for it.

'You got any more of them CDs to sell?' he asked me, changing the subject.

'Nah – Gussie's gonna do some more this weekend – should have some next week . . .'

'Good,' replied Jit, 'I could use the money . . .'

I was going to say something but Jit saw Grace and Hannah coming towards us and got all funny.

'I'm goin' to the toilets to sort out my hair,' he said.

'Never bothered you before,' I said.

'See you in class,' he replied, running off before Hannah and Grace reached us.

They watched him go and shook their heads.

'Strange boy,' said Grace.

'Easy Grace – don't upset the football hooligans – they might attack us like wolves goin' after elks . . .' joked Hannah.

'Yeah – what the hell was Black on about?' I asked, not giving Jit another thought.

'Dunno – he's a funny old git,' laughed Hannah.

'Bit harsh on us though,' I said.

'I thought that,' said Grace. 'I mean the other team were being racist – so why should we have to apologise?'

'Exactly,' I told them. 'Seems to me like it's different rules for them schools, you get me?'

'No there aren't,' said Hannah.

'So you explain it then . . .'

Hannah looked at me and grinned. 'OK – I *will* then . . . er . . . *later* . . . when I've asked me mum,' she said.

When I got home that evening I spent an hour sitting in front of the telly, not really paying attention to what I was watching. Ruby turned up around half-past five with a load of shopping bags and slumped down on the sofa next to me.

'*More* clothes?' I asked.

'None of your business,' she told me.

'How many do you need, man?'

She looked at me like I was an insect.

'I *change* my clothes – *every* day – not like you, you *dutty* tramp.'

I was about to answer back when my Gramps walked in and sat down too.

'I see yuh a buy more clothes,' he said to Ruby, who groaned.

'Leave it out, Gramps – he's just been saying the same thing. I'm a *girl* – I need to have clothes . . .'

Gramps shook his head and let out a little sigh. 'Back when I was growin' up in Kingston, me 'ave *one* shirt pon mi back and *one* shoes pon mi foot . . .'

I grinned at Ruby. It was a story that he always told us.

'So you never had no trousers then?' I asked.

'*Eh?*'

'*Trousers*, Gramps. You walk around in your boxer shorts . . . ?'

'You likkle *raas* – of course mi 'ave trouser – two of dem . . . but we never 'ave money like de yout' dem today. You two dunno yuh born, man. Spoil fe true . . .' he replied, shaking his head again.

'Well we ain't in Jamaica,' said Ruby. 'This is *England* and a girl needs to have clothes . . .'

Gramps let out a little giggle.

'*Inglan*? Yuh father should 'ave moved yuh *raas* to Jamaica, man. None a dem pickney spoilt like yuh . . .'

Pickney means 'kids' and Gramps went on to tell us how there was no discipline in English schools which meant that kids had no morals nowadays.

I just kept on grinning at my sister as Gramps went off on one, not stopping to see if we were even listening.

'One cuff pon dem 'ead an' dem soon hush dem mout',' he mumbled.

Gussie walked in just as Gramps was winding up. He told me to come up to his room.

'What for?' I asked, as Gramps turned his attention to the telly and the news.

'Never mind – just get yer skinny backside up the stairs, man,' replied Gussie.

'Which one of you is helpin' with the dinner tonight?' asked Ruby.

'We'll toss a coin,' said Gussie.

'You best do an' all. I ain't doin' it all on my own again. You wan' eat, yuh best help wid it . . .' she warned, sounding just like my mum.

I groaned and got up out of the comfort of my seat. I followed Gussie up the stairs to the first floor and walked into his room, which was at the back of the house. It was a mess, with clothes all over the floor and empty mugs and plates everywhere. There were CDs stacked high on a shelf next to a neat little Sony sound system too and on the floor stood two massive speakers that weren't connected up.

'Where'd you get them?' I asked about the speakers.

'Mate,' replied Gussie, as usual. It was like his stock answer to everything.

'So what do you want?' I said, not that I was in any

hurry to go back downstairs and peel potatoes or whatever it was that Ruby had lined up for me.

'Phones, my boy,' said Gussie with a grin, putting on a posh accent. 'Mobile communication devices especially for the youths of today. Super, what?'

'Just shut up and let me see them,' I told him.

He picked up a bag from his bed and unzipped it, pulling out a mobile phone. Handing it to me, he threw the bag back down onto the bed. I looked at the silver handset and flipped it open. It was a top of the range Motorola with a camera, Blue-tooth and everything. The only thing it didn't have was video phone.

'Man – this is cool,' I said, turning it over in my hands. It was so light.

'Them things ain't nothing,' said Gussie. 'There's a new range about to come out, even better . . . Raj is getting me one as soon as they get released.'

'How many you got?' I asked.

'Six – all with the chargers and hands-free kits too. Should be easy to get rid of,' he said.

'How much?' I asked.

Gussie shrugged. 'Up to you what you charge for them . . .' he said, looking away.

'Nah – I meant how much do you want?'

He picked up the bag again and tipped out the rest.

Then he sat down on his bed and played with one of his rings.

'I got 'em for nothing,' he told me. 'I told you – they was extra stock that Raj wanted rid of and he owed me for some stuff anyways . . .'

I frowned at him.

'Something wrong with them?' I asked, getting worried.

'Don't be a knob – why would I take a load of dodgy phones? Ain't exactly good business, is it?'

I thought about it for a minute and realised that he was right. He wouldn't have taken them if they were messed up. As the thought dawned on me, Gussie told me what he wanted.

'Just give us fifty for 'em,' he said.

'Each?'

'Nah – for the lot, baby brother. And don't say that I never look after you.'

I was going to protest but greed took over and I realised that I would make loads of money on them. I looked at my brother who shrugged again, in a 'take it or leave it' kind of way.

'You got a deal,' I told him, grinning like a fool.

I ran up to my room, got out my stash of savings and counted out fifty quid. Then I ran back downstairs to give it to Gussie, half expecting him to have changed his mind or laugh and say that it was all a wind-up. The phones were worth one hundred and fifty pounds each, *minimum*, in the shops which meant that I could sell them for seventy-five quid each, no problem. It was the deal of the century, the bargain of the new millennium. I was well happy. I handed my money to Gussie and grabbed the phones, just as I heard the door bell ring.

EIGHT

'DEAN! Someone to see you,' shouted Ruby.

I stashed the phones in my room and ran down the stairs wondering who it was. I thought it might be Hannah but when I got to the front door Jit was standing there. He looked really embarrassed and he had a bag with him.

'Yes, Jit – come on in to the madhouse,' I said, shutting the door behind him.

'Thanks,' he replied, walking into the hallway and putting his bag down.

'I . . . er . . . need a favour, bro,' he said, looking down at his feet.

'You need that homework you missed last week?' I asked but he shook his head.

'Nah – it's kinda something else.'

'What?' I asked.

'Er . . . I was hoping . . . I need a place to stay, man.'

I looked at him and I swear I saw tears in his eyes, so I told him to come through to the living room. My head was going in all sorts of directions, trying to work out what was up. Jit sat down, looking even more embarrassed than before.

'Evenin',' said my Gramps.

'Yeah . . . evenin',' replied Jit, quietly.

'You wanna tell me what's going on?' I asked.

Jit tried to smile at me but he couldn't. I heard my mum come through the door as I stood where I was, looking at my best mate.

'You best come upstairs,' I said, realising that he wouldn't talk in front of my family.

My mum walked in and smiled at everyone. She saw Jit and grinned. 'Hi Jit, how are you? I haven't seen you in ages.'

'Hi Mrs Chambers,' he replied.

'Mum – me and Jit are gonna go upstairs for a chat. Is it OK if he stays for dinner?'

My mum smiled warmly. 'Of course it is, sweetheart.'

Normally I would have been embarrassed at her calling me that in front of a mate but I was too worried about Jit to care. I went upstairs and Jit followed. Once we were in my room, I asked him what was up.

'My mum's been seein' this bloke and he don't like me so I don't want to go home,' he told me.

'What – has he been hitting you?' I asked, getting angry.

'Nah – nothing like that. He just gets drunk all the

time and swears at me. Mum don't say nothing either.'

'That's messed up, man,' I told him.

'Last night I didn't even *go* home,' Jit said, playing with his hands and not looking at me.

'You what? So where did you sleep . . . ?'

'In the park . . .'

I sat back in shock and more anger.

'Nah, nah, nah – that ain't happenin' man,' I said, shaking my head.

'I forgot my keys and Mum was at work. When I knocked on the door he told me to get lost. I walked around for ages and tried again about eleven but they didn't answer the door.'

'Didn't your mum notice you weren't there in the morning?' I asked.

Jit shrugged.

'I never see her in the morning. She's always asleep because she works late and goes out and that . . .'

He saw the look in my eyes and shook his head.

'It ain't her fault, Dean. It's him . . . Micky. I just don't wanna go home. I mean he let me in today but he threatened me, too. Told me he'd do me if I told Mum what happened . . .'

'Have you told your mum?' I asked.

Jit shook his head.

'I just grabbed some stuff and walked out. Mum's working till two in the morning anyway...'

'That's a crap shift, man.'

'It's only 'cause the store opens twenty-four hours now... she used to finish at ten before... and it ain't her fault,' he repeated.

I didn't know what else to say. I knew that things were hard for Jit at home but I didn't realise how bad they were. It kind of made me understand why he went nuts sometimes – I know I would have. I was so lucky to be close to my family. Sometimes it's easy to forget how lucky you really are, man. In the end I told him that we'd eat some food and that afterwards he should tell my mum.

'I don't wanna lie to her, bro' – that ain't right,' I told him.

'OK,' he said, without complaining.

We *could* have lied and said that he was staying over because we had arranged it but my mum can spot a lie from ten miles away. She's got this radar thing going on with her senses. And she would be hurt too. We went downstairs and sat in front of the telly as Gussie helped Ruby sort out the dinner. It was supposed to have been my turn but he didn't complain. Not in front of Mum, anyway.

We ate with my entire family, like we always did on Friday nights. My dad turned up around seven o'clock

and by the time we sat down at the table I was starving.
Jit sat next to me and after a while he cheered up a bit,
especially when my Gramps started going on about his
medical problems, like he always did.

'Yuh 'ave pepper sauce, Pearl?' he asked my mum.

She passed it across and Gramps opened it and poured
it over his rice and chicken like he was pouring ketchup.
My dad had bought the pepper sauce over from the West
Indies and it was extra hot, like a grenade going off in
your mouth. But Gramps didn't even feel it. At one point
he even put *more* on his food. I asked Jit if the food was
nice, which was a stupid question because he was eating
it so quickly that he must have liked it. He swallowed a
mouthful and nodded.

''S'great,' he said. 'I like hot food.'

My dad laughed.

'You wanna try the pepper sauce, Jit – it's seriously
hot.'

'Why's it called Ooh Mi Raas!,' I asked my dad, even
though I knew what it meant.

'Not at the table, Clem,' said my mum.

'Why not?' asked Gussie. 'Gramps talks like that all
the time and, anyway, it ain't rude . . .'

Gramps smiled at Jit.

'Mi used to 'ave one Indian fren a school, y'know.'

Jit looked at me and grinned.

'Really?' he said.

'Yeah man – 'im name Guptal Patel – one wicked fas' bowler . . . im' coulda lick dung dem wicket . . .'

This time Jit looked confused.

'He's talking about cricket,' said my dad, as Gramps carried on eating, like he hadn't actually started a conversation.

'So . . . why *is* it called Ooh Mi Raas!,' asked Ruby. 'It's a stupid name for pepper sauce.'

'OK – seeing as Gramps hasn't bought up toilet humour at the table – I'll have to,' relented my mum, grinning like a kid.

'Yuh waan get a extra hot sauce, nex' time. Dis one is a'right but it nuh keep yuh reg'lar like dem one in Jamaica . . .'

'It's from Antigua, Dad,' said my dad, winking at me and Jit.

'*Antigua*? Is dat why it 'ave such a stupid name?'

My dad started laughing.

'The name, if you translate it, means "Oh my arse!" because of the laxative effect that the peppers have . . .' he explained to Jit.

'It makes you shit yourself if you . . .' began my brother.

'*GUSSIE!*' shouted my mum, though she immediately cracked up along with everyone else, apart from Gramps.

'Is no wonder mi bone dem ache and mi 'ave piles . . .' said Gramps.

'*Ehhh, Gramps*!' said Ruby. 'That's nasty . . .'

Gramps smiled and winked at me and Jit.

'Jus' like yuh hairdo,' he whispered with a grin.

'*MUM* . . . !' protested Ruby but my mum was laughing along too.

My dad watched Jit clear his plate and then asked him if he wanted some more.

'Yes please, Mr Chambers,' replied Jit, looking more than happy.

My dad took his plate and gave him a load more food, before filling up my plate and his own too. He picked up the bottle of sauce.

'You want some?' asked my dad.

'Er . . . nah – it's spicy enough for me,' said Jit.

'He don't wanna spend the rest of the evening in our shi—'

'Gussie, I told you – *shut it*!' said my mum.

'Course, back in my day a bwoi woulda get lick dung if 'im cheek 'im muddah so . . .' said Gramps.

'Don't worry about it, Gramps,' replied my mum, glaring at Gussie. 'It could a still 'appen here too . . .'

'I was only jokin' Mum . . .' said Gussie.

'We neveh tell joke at de table,' started Gramps. 'Cah we would a get . . .'

'*Lick dung*!' said my dad, acting like a kid.

Gramps pulled out his lower set of false teeth and cleaned them with his forefinger before putting them back into his mouth. He shook his head, muttered to himself and carried on with his dinner.

Afterwards we told Mum about what was up with Jit and she took him into the kitchen and spoke to him for ages as I watched telly with my sister. Dad and Gussie went off to work and Gramps was sitting in the front room listening to the BBC World Service on his old radio. When my mum and Jit returned, he was smiling and my mum told me that he was going to stay the night and that she'd phoned his mum at work to talk to her.

'Everything's going to be fine,' she told me, sitting down on the sofa.

'You OK, bro?' I asked Jit.

'Yeah – I spoke to Mum . . .' he said, smiling at me.

'So it's sorted?'

'Yeah – she's coming round tomorrow afternoon.'

'I've got some of that toffee ice cream,' said my mum. 'You want to get it out of the freezer, Dean?'

I smiled and went into the kitchen, relieved that my best mate was OK.

NINE

Jit was waiting for me outside his house the following Monday, looking happier than I'd seen him in ages. His mum had picked him up on the Saturday and spent half an hour chatting with my mum. She'd given her boyfriend the push, she said, and I went round on Sunday evening to chill out.

The next day we walked down to Grace's as usual and caught the bus to school, all of us in a good mood, even though I hadn't done the poem for the school paper. It turned out that I didn't need to either because when I saw Hannah at registration she told me that the last article was going to be written by Mr Black.

'He's writing something about the football thing last week,' she told me. 'About racism and how to react to it properly.'

'Saved *my* skin,' I pointed out, but Hannah shook her head.

'Not exactly – he said that he still wants you to write it for the next one.'

'Yeah,' I replied, 'but that's not for a few weeks is it?'

'Gives you time to get on with it then,' said Hannah.

'No problem, Sister Aitch.'

I heard Grace yelp behind me and turned to find her bent over Jit's knee with her bag round her neck and her hair all over the shop.

'Yo, Jit – not in the classroom, man,' I laughed.

'Ehh! What you two doin'?' asked Suky.

'I was trying to get her bag,' said Jit, going all red, as Grace straightened herself up and stood there, looking like someone had painted her face with raspberry juice too.

'Er . . .' she began but Hannah just held up her hand.

'Don't even try to explain,' she said. 'I don't know what you were doing but there's laws, *y'know* . . . ?'

'OK – quiet everyone,' said Mrs Dooher.

'Miss! Grace and Jit are trying to have sex . . .' shouted a lad called Marco.

Mrs Dooher tried to look all serious but she couldn't manage it and she broke out into a grin.

'I'm sure they're not,' she told Marco.

'But I seen them – Grace was all over him,' added Marco's twin brother, Milorad.

'You saw them, Milorad. Not seen . . .' corrected Mrs Dooher.

'But I did seen, Miss,' said Milorad.

'Oh – never mind – just keep quiet and pay attention.

And Grace, can you at least keep your hands to yourself until you're in your next lesson? I'd much rather Mr Herbert had to deal with this kind of thing . . .'

'I wasn't doing anything, Miss,' Grace protested.

'Yeah – we were just messing about,' said Jit, before turning to Marco.

'I'm gonna batter you,' he said.

'*JIT!*' shouted Mrs Dooher.

'Oh I'm sorry Miss,' replied Jit, turning back to Marco. 'I shall jolly well bash you on the nose, my good fellow,' he told him, in a stupid voice.

'OK – enough. I'm too old for this rubbish.'

'Just think, Miss,' said Hannah. 'If he'd have only asked you out, that Paul McFartney or whatever, when you were a young woman – you'd be rich and famous now . . .'

'Yes, yes, Hannah. Thank you for reminding me . . .' said Mrs Dooher, smiling warmly.

'Tropical islands, yachts. Your own chef . . . just think,' continued Hannah.

'A *gun*,' added Mrs Dooher, jokingly.

Hannah said 'oops' and shut up.

I spent most of the morning thinking about who I was going to try and sell the mobile phones to. I'd decided to ask for seventy pounds for each of them, which I thought was the deal of the year considering that they were more than double that in the shops. I'd brought one with me to school, and every few minutes I kept opening my bag and having a secret look at it. I didn't even tell Jit but I was going to eventually. All I wanted to do first was test the water. Do a bit of market research and that. My first option was trying a lad called Dilip who was in my class. His old man was loaded and they owned a load of take-away shops all over the city. He had a wicked phone already but I knew that I could tempt him with another one. Especially at the price I was giving him. I thought that I might even be able to sell him a couple of them – one for him and one for his brother, Nital, who was in the year above us. I finally got hold of Dilip at lunch, when he was standing in line for food. I went over as he was piling his plate high with chips. There was a slice of pizza underneath but it had been covered with the potatoes.

'Yes, Dilip – what a gwaan, man?' I asked him, a big smile on my face.

Dilip looked around, like he didn't think that I was talking to him, even though I had used his name.

'You talkin' to *me* guy?' he asked, in his whiny voice.

'Yeah, man. How's it hangin' homeboy?'

'Safe, innit,' he told me, grabbing about ten sachets of ketchup.

I took a plate and put some chips on it, along with a

piece of dry looking chicken that was supposed to be tandoori. It was bright red, like that Ferrari colour, and as soon as it hit my plate, it left stains on the white surface. Nice. I was going to complain but I didn't. School dinners had got me into enough trouble already.

'Anyway, bro, I was *thinking*,' I said.

'Yeah?' replied Dilip.

'That *mobile* you got – it's kinda rude, man.'

For a moment Dilip looked worried, like I was about to tax his raas or something. I grinned at him, so that he'd calm down and in my head I cussed him for thinking I was a thief. Talk about stereotype city, man.

'I ain't gonna *rob* you,' I told him. 'I just wondered if you was in the market for a new one, is all.'

Dilip shrugged.

'Happy with the one I got, man,' he told me.

'I'm happy with mine too but why settle for the *Ford Fiesta* when you can have the *Mercedes* . . . ?'

'You what?' he asked, looking puzzled.

'I got these top of the *range* things, man. Motorola with *everything* and open to every network. Man, dem tings open to some networks ain't even *exist* yet, you get me?'

'But I don't *want* a new phone,' he repeated.

'Listen – right *now* you don't want one but when one of the other kids gets one, then you'll feel stink. You gotta ask yerself what you is goin' to *be*, Dilip, my brother. A *leader* or a *follower*, you get me?'

Dilip walked off with his tray of food and I followed, sitting down next to him.

'I'm offering you a less than half price phone – the best on the market. At least have a look at it nuh man.'

Dilip looked at one or two of the other lads at the table, all his friends, and then looked at me.

'Open to anything?' he asked.

I smiled. Just fling out the line and reel dem fishes in, I thought to myself.

'Every single one. I got them off a mate who owns a shop, man. Pure *legit*.'

'Lemme see then, bro',' he replied. I unzipped my bag and pulled out the phone and straight away, I could tell that he wanted one. His eyes widened and lit up like there was floodlights behind them.

'*See*? Nice, innit?'

'Yeah, man . . . I seen one of these in the shop. Hundred and seventy notes . . .'

'Well that's even more of a saving for yer, Dilip. I'm *only* asking *seventy* . . .'

'What's wrong with it?' asked Dilip, warily.

'Nuttin' man. I got another *five* waiting at home.'

'So why is they so *cheap*?' he said.

'End of line – stock clearance. My guy, Raj at Raj Electronics gave them to me.'

'That the shop on East Park Road?' asked Dilip.

'Yeah – that's the one – up the road from your dad's place.'

'I know him so if they're dodgy, I'll find out,' he warned.

'Then what you got to *lose*? I'm kinda acting as his agent anyways,' I lied. 'He need to shift some stock – *off the books*, you get me?'

I winked at him, like it was our big secret. The last bit made Dilip change his mind, I reckon. He smiled and told me about how his dad had to do things off the books sometimes.

'Get tax too much otherwise, innit,' he told me.

'So what you *saying* – we's looking out for the small *biznizz*, innit?' I replied, turning on the charm.

'OK, Dean – I'll get the money tomorrow but they better be all right . . .'

'Come Dilip, man. Would I have your legs up?'

He thought about it for a minute and then told me he'd see me tomorrow.

'Ask around too, man. Anyone else you know wants one – just send 'em my way. But keep it under wraps, man.'

He nodded.

'I'm serious, bro'. Pure MI5 business a gwaan . . .'

I stood up and walked over to where Jit and Imtiaz

were sitting, a big smile playing on my face. Damn, I was good, I told myself.

'What you smiling at?' asked Jit as I took my usual seat.

'Just thinking 'bout how I might have to go into stock-brokering or some shit when I'm older . . .'

'Eh? You don't even like maths,' said Imi. 'How are you gonna sell stocks and shares?'

'Ain't about maths, is it?' I said, even though I didn't have a clue what I was on about.

'So what's it all about then?' asked Imi, getting on his high horse.

'You can either sell or you can't,' I told him. 'And I'm the daddy of salesmen, man. The bona fide, *numero uno*, you get me?'

'You eat summat funny?' asked Jit, giving me a strange look. 'Other than a dictionary, I mean . . .'

'I'll tell you later,' I said, as I saw Mr Herbert walk into the dining hall.

'YOW! HERBERT BWOI!!!' I shouted, leaning down under the table, so that he wouldn't see me.

Everyone in the hall stopped for moment, waiting to see if someone would get into trouble. When nothing happened, they started talking again. I went further under the table, my knee slipping on a soggy chip that was on the floor.

'DUTTY HERBERT, BWOI! Is where you get that tie . . . ?' I shouted.

This time there was total silence. I thought about not carrying on but the stupid part of my head beat up the sensible bit.

'The thing so nasty, it even make yuh mother cry . . . !' I said, finishing my little rhyme.

'*WHO SAID THAT*!' bellowed Herbert, as the other kids started laughing.

I heard Jit snigger and stayed under the table, getting ready for the big finale. I put on a really deep voice.

'*FEE FI FO FUM . . . I smell a dutty Herbert man, Man so nasty he never cleans . . . Only polishes his head with Mr Sheen.*'

My voice had been amplified by being under the table and the whole hall went up in laughter, as I scrambled out from my hiding place and took my seat. As I did that Jit and Imi stood up so that I wouldn't get seen. Mr Herbert was so red in the face that I thought he was going to burst like a giant strawberry. He was looking in my direction too but in the end he stomped out of the hall because he couldn't prove that it had been me who'd dissed him.

'You're nuts, man,' laughed Imi.

'Least I got 'em,' I replied, grinning.

TEN

Dilip bought one of the phones at morning break the next day. I tried to sell him one for his brother but he told me that he was going to wait and see if his was OK first.

'Your loss,' I told him. 'Once in a lifetime bargain, man.'

Jit came up as he was walking away and asked me what I was up to.

'Sellin' phones, bro,' I told him.

I opened my bag and got out another one, handing it to him. He looked at it, flipped it open and whistled.

'Nice . . .'

'I got five left – you can have one if you like . . .'

'*Serious?*'

I grinned.

'Not to keep for yourself, you fool. I'm selling 'em for seventy notes. You sell that one, give me a tenner and you're laughing,' I said.

Jit flipped it open and shut a few more times.

'It's worth more than a tenner, bro,' he said.

'You're looking it in the mouth,' I replied.

'You *what*?' he said, giving me a funny look.

'The Gift Horse.'

I don't know whether he got the reference but he smiled and said thank you.

'There's gotta be summat up with them, though.'

I shook my head

'Nuttin' man. Gussie got 'em from Raj – *you know*, the one that owns the phone shop . . . ?'

'Yeah – I know him – drives that big Audi.'

'Well he had to get rid of a few, off the books,' I said, before winking at him.

'*Cool*. Dunno who I'm gonna sell it to though. How many of the kids at school got seventy quid to play with?'

I smiled at him.

'*Plenty*. You's forgettin' all the posh kids that live round Grace's way . . .'

'Oh yeah,' he said, like he'd only just heard about them for the first time.

'That's where your skill as a salesman comes in,' I told him.

'Oh, that's what you was on about yesterday. I thought you'd been licking rock, man.'

'Never . . . and walk around like I'm from outer space? *Leave dat* . . . !'

We chatted for a bit longer and then walked slowly towards our next lesson. Robert and Wesley were waiting outside the classroom when we got there, *still* talking about that lame book.

'So what's new with the flute of kings then?' I asked.

Robert shut up quickly and looked down at his feet but Wesley didn't realise that I was having a laugh and started to tell me.

'Tar, the talking rat, has turned to the Dark Way,' he said.

'Nah . . . !' I said, pretending to be really shocked.

'I'm afraid so. He's taken the flute from the princess. She was sleeping and he stole in and spirited it away and now it's with the Dark Lord and . . .'

'What about Ganglefart the Goblin?' I asked.

Wesley looked at me strangely.

'I don't think that there is a Ganglefart, unless of course you've read more of it than me . . .'

'He's having a joke at our expense,' said Robert.

'*Oh dearie me*,' said Jit, sarcastically.

'I ain't,' I told them. 'I'm just exercising my imagination – you know, making up my own characters and that . . .'

'Oh right,' said Wesley, looking at Robert.

'I suppose that's really rather clever,' admitted Robert. 'I never thought of that.'

'You should write your own,' I said.

I wasn't joking either. Not *completely*. Robert and Wesley had read every fantasy book going. They were like experts on good and evil, witches and sorcerers and that.

'I am,' said Robert, going red.

'What's it called?' I asked, as Jit pretended to yawn.

'It's a bit of a steal actually. I'm writing a further adventure of Princess Wondlebarn . . .'

'You mean Cat Deeley?'

'Well yes, I suppose. Only recently my visual image of the princess has changed somewhat . . .'

'Who to . . . ?' I asked, trying not to crack up.

'I'd rather not say,' he told me, going even redder than he already had and looking over my shoulder.

I turned to see Hannah and Grace walking towards us.

'*Hiya boys*,' they said together, in American accents.

'Yo, sistas,' I replied. 'Roberto's writing a *book* . . .'

'*Are you?*' asked Grace in a silly, girlie voice. '*Really* . . . ?'

'Erm . . . well . . .' began Robert.

'He is,' Wesley replied for him. 'It's a fantasy and it's about . . .'

'Goblins and dwarves . . . ?' asked Grace.

'*Yes!*' said Robert, a bit too loudly.

'Excellent,' replied Grace. She held out her hand and touched Robert's sleeve, leaning towards his face. 'You will remember *liddle old moi* when you're rich, won't you?' she asked.

Robert pulled his arm away and I swear his legs were shaking. He looked at his friend before replying.

'Of . . . of . . . c.c.course . . .' he stuttered.

'Awfully *nice* of you,' said Grace, looking at Hannah, who had a bored expression on her face.

'Better go,' she said. 'Lovely to talk to you again, Roberto . . .'

Robert mumbled something back to her and walked off into class, with Wesley behind him. I looked at my friends and shook my head.

'You lot are so mean, man,' I told them.

'What? You started it,' said Jit. 'Talkin' bout nonsense and that . . .'

'I was being *nice*,' said Grace.

'Yeah, right. Like I believe you . . .' said Hannah.

'I *was*,' she protested. 'Those poor boys are always getting grief – I was just being their friend . . .'

'Bein' a div more like,' said Jit.

'Smelly, poo pants . . .' replied Grace, walking into the classroom.

Jit's face fell.

'She's only playing with you, Jit,' said Hannah, looking bemused. 'God, sometimes I wonder whether boys have got any brains at all . . .'

Jit sold the second phone as we were walking back to my house, later on. We were walking past a Caribbean takeaway that my aunt ran and as we turned the corner into a side street I heard someone call my name.

'Dean . . .' came the whisper.

I looked behind me and saw Dilip.

'Easy Dilip – what a gwaan?' I asked him, wondering why he was speaking so softly. Jit didn't bother to hold his thoughts in though.

'What you whisperin' for you knob?' he asked loudly.

'I got someone else, innit. Wants a ting . . .' replied Dilip, looking embarrassed.

'What ting?' said Jit.

'A phone, bro . . .' Dilip told us.

I smiled and shook my head.

'See? Me done tell you you'd want another one . . .' I told him.

'Still can't see why you is whisperin' like a girl,' said Jit.

'But . . . Dean said to keep it hush-hush, innit,' replied Dilip. 'I'm just bein' careful . . .'

'You sound like you is asking us for *drugs* or summat,' I said.

'Sorry, man . . .' replied Dilip, looking worried.

'Ain't no one around to hear us,' I said. 'We ain't in school, man.'

Dilip looked around like he had only just realised that we weren't still at school. The idiot.

'Safe,' he said, once he was sure that no one was listening.

'We ain't sellin' crack, you div,' said Jit, breaking all the rules of selling. You didn't call your potential customer names. I realised that I was going to have to step in to save the sale.

'Jit's got one,' I told Dilip. 'Same price as the other one . . .'

'Yeah . . . I got the notes on me,' said Dilip, still trying to keep his voice down.

I looked at Jit.

'*What?*' he said.

'The *phone*, Jit. Get the phone out man.'

'Oh yeah,' replied Jit, catching on with the same speed that a tortoise uses to catch up with a hare. Or a Nissan Micra with a Subaru Impreza.

Jit pulled the phone and the bits that went with it out of his bag and handed them to Dilip. Dilip waited for a moment and then held out his hand like he was going to shake Jit's.

'What you doin' you fool?' asked Jit.

'Givin' you the money, innit,' said Dilip.

Jit took what Dilip had in his hands. He had folded the notes into a tight little square and Jit had to straighten them out. I watched him do it and then decided to play a little joke.

'POLICE!' I shouted.

Dilip's face dropped and he looked like he had just

pooped his pants, whilst Jit panicked and tried to shove the money down his trousers. Both of them were looking around for the police. When they realised that they were safe, both of them turned their attention to me. I just shrugged and grinned at them.

'Teach you not to be paranoid,' I said, shaking my head. 'Fools . . .'

Dilip put the phone in his bag and told us he was going.

'Later,' I said, just as my auntie came out of her shop.

'*DEAN*!' she shouted at the top of her voice. 'Is what you doin' messin 'bout outside my business?'

'Hi Auntie Sandra,' I said.

'Better not be doin' nuttin' wrong,' she told me, before eyeing up Jit.

'Who ah dis?' she asked.

'This is my best mate, Jit,' I told her.

'You wan' come in an' nyam some food?' she asked, smiling now.

'An' get beat by me mum for not eatin' at home? *Nah* – I'll check you another time, Auntie,' I told her.

'Anytime,' she said, looking around and then cussing a wino who was sitting on the pavement, across the street.

'*Eeedjat* . . .' she called to him, before going back into her shop.

ELEVEN

Things started to go wrong the next day. I was walking from History to English when I felt a hand grab my jumper from behind. My legs started buckling as I got dragged backwards into the toilets. When the hands let go of me I straightened myself out and turned to see Jason Patel grinning at me. He's a weird looking brother, Jason, with red hair and red freckles on light, almost yellow skin. His nose is too long for his face and his eyes are like little piggy things and when he smiles, he's seriously ugly. I'm talking scare-the-living-poo-out-of-a-serial-killer *butt* ugly. I looked at him for a moment and then looked away, my eyes hitting the floor.

'What did I tell you?' he asked, poking me in the chest with his finger.

Now there's some things that I can handle, like being punched or kicked. You know that's going to hurt and you get it over with. But when Jason poked me in the chest I started to get really angry. It didn't hurt, it just stung a little bit, but it was so irritating. And then he did it over and over again. I was dying to hit him but I knew that if I did he would batter me, good and proper. In the end I played the tough nut and just shrugged at him.

'Dunno,' I said.

'WHAT DID I TELL YOU . . . ?' he shouted, making me flinch.

'Summat 'bout not sellin' nuttin' or summat . . .' I replied.

'Exactly,' he said, calming down a bit. 'And what do I hear you been doing?'

'Sellin' shit . . .' I admitted.

'Yep – so either you don't care 'cause you is so hard or you is trying to diss me, man . . .' he said.

'Nah . . . I just forgot,' I said, trying to style it out. Yeah, right.

Jason grabbed my jumper and head-butted the side of my face. He would have butted my nose but I turned my head. My ear was stinging and I felt light-headed but I didn't fall over or cry. I just stood my ground, tears and all and had a quick flash in my head of Gussie kicking the shit out of him for me.

'You won't forget that . . .' he told me, grabbing my bag from my shoulder and opening it. I didn't try to stop him – I'm not that stupid.

He rummaged around before pulling out one of the phones. Luckily I had only bought one with me. He would have taken the lot otherwise.

'That'll do,' he said.

'They's seventy notes,' I told him.

'Yeah,' he grinned, 'I'll write you a cheque, man . . .'

'But they don't belong to me,' I said quickly, without thinking. 'They belong to this man up East Park Road . . .'

'*And* . . . ?' he asked, grinning again, his face creasing like someone had squashed his head down.

'Well he's gonna want his money . . .'

'You threatening me?' he asked, his grin disappearing.

'Nah . . . I'm just sayin' that the bwoi is gonna want his dough . . .'

Jason looked at the phone in his hands and then back at me.

'Tell him that he can ask me himself,' he said, acting all brave.

'OK, then,' I said.

He turned to go, throwing my bag to the floor, but then he turned, walked up to me and slapped me on the same ear that he had caught with his head.

'Next time you'd better listen to me,' he said, before walking out of the toilets.

I grabbed my bag and walked into one of the cubicles, locked the door and sat down on the lid, trying to calm down. Then I thought about what I was going to do about Jason.

* * *

In the end I didn't tell anyone about what Jason had done. I decided that it would be easier to leave it and get my own back some other way. It was the right decision in the end, too, only I didn't know it at the time. I sold the last three phones over the next few days, and when I counted up the money, along with the tenner that Jit gave me for his phone, I'd made two hundred and ninety quid. It would have been more but for Jason Patel, the knob. Still, it was a lot of money and I decided that I was going to buy turntables with it. I'd always wanted them and I told Gussie that he was going to have to cover for me when they arrived so that my mum wouldn't get funny about where the money had come from. Gussie told me that he'd say he had lent me the money from his wages, and got them from a friend. I rang up Jit on the Friday night and told him to come round for dinner. He turned up about two minutes after I'd put the phone down, with an overnight bag.

'Mind if I stay over?' he asked, putting his bag down on my bed.

'Looks like you've already decided for me,' I said, smiling. 'It's cool.'

'What's for food, man?' he asked, looking excited.

'Same as last time, I think.'

'Wicked . . .' replied Jit.

'Come – let's go and eat and then we's got some *research* to do on the Internet, man.'

Jit gave me a strange look.

'What for?'

'I'm buying some decks, man,' I told him.

'Decks . . . ?'

'Yeah – DJ tings . . . we can share them though . . .'

Jit thought about it for a moment and then smiled at me.

'Gets better and better,' he said.

Gramps spent the entire meal telling us about the time that he pitched up in a place called Studio One with the owner and a bloke called Prince Buster, whilst they were making some old Ska tunes or something. Ska's like the first version of reggae music, I think, but I didn't ask. I just nodded along, as Gramps told us about this girl they used to call *Mash-Mout Lorna* because she had no teeth. My sister, whose middle name is Lorna, was going mental because me and Gussie were ripping her about it and in the end my dad had to tell us to stop because she was about to run out of the room. Gramps didn't even notice. Instead he told us about meeting Bob Marley instead. I reckon he makes up half of his stories about the Jamaican music industry but I don't care because they're normally *well* funny.

After we had eaten, me and Jit had to load up the dishwasher and then we grabbed a drink each and headed up to my room. I signed into my server and hit the Google button. Then I typed 'DJ *equipment*' into the search panel and hit '*search*'. The page came up in about half a second and I started to read down the list of online shops, reading out the little promotional lines to Jit. After a few minutes I clicked one of the links and the page for the shop downloaded onto my computer screen. As soon as it was done I realised that I had a problem. You can't buy online with cash. I told this to Jit who just shrugged and took the mouse from me, clicking on a picture of some really expensive Technics decks.

'We can't get them,' I told him. 'They cost too much – I've got two twenty, maybe thirty, max.'

'I thought you had more dough than that?' asked Jit.

'Yeah, I have,' I told him, 'but I don't wanna spend it all, man. There's other things I need to keep it for . . .'

'Cool,' said Jit. 'You can put in a maximum spend amount in this box here.' He pointed it out with the mouse.

'I'll just type in two thirty,' he added.

'I've gotta go talk to Gussie first,' I said, getting out of my seat. Jit jumped straight in.

'Cool – I'll just check out a few options,' he said, like he was some kind of shopping expert.

I went downstairs to find Gussie, who had the night off from my dad's bar. He was in the lounge, lying on the sofa watching rubbish on the telly.

'I need a favour, bro,' I told him.

He looked at me for a bit and then turned his attention back to the TV.

'Gussie . . . ?'

'What . . . ?'

'I need to borrow your Switch card ting . . .'

'You what?' he said, sitting up. 'Is what kind of nonsense yuh a chat 'bout?'

I pulled the wad of notes that were in my pocket out and showed them to him.

'Not for nuttin',' I told him. 'I've got the money, man . . .'

'*Raas*,' said Gussie, in surprise. 'That all from them phones . . . ?'

'Yeah,' I said, suspiciously. 'You said I could do what I wanted with them . . .'

Gussie grinned.

'Relax, man. I don't want a bigger cut, baby bro. What you need my card for?'

I told him and he nodded, telling me that as long as he could use the decks too, then he would lend me his card. I gave him two hundred and thirty quid in cash which he put in his back pocket.

'Is there enough money in your account?' I asked.

'*Yeah man* . . . me have money, y'know. Besides it's the least I can do considering . . .'

Only I didn't really think about the last bit that he said because I was already turning to run back upstairs, excited about getting the turntables. Bad move.

Jit was still looking at turntable and mixer combinations when I got back to my room and he showed me a load that were all around the right price. I took my seat from him and went into another online shop and then another, trying to find the best deal. In the end we settled on a pair of Vestax decks which were belt driven, not direct drive, which is the best for mixing tunes. But we weren't exactly about to become big time DJs so we didn't need the best anyway. The mixer was by Gemini and in the end we got it all for less than two hundred and thirty quid. We even got a free pair of headphones thrown in and I entered Gussie's card details as quickly as I could. They were next day delivery too, although we had ordered them too late in the day and when I got the confirmation e-mail it said that they would be dispatched the next day, Saturday, which meant that they'd probably arrive by Monday. I was well excited, so much so that I forgot all about Jason Patel. Instead we played on my games console until about two in the morning.

TWELVE

The next day me and Jit went round to Grace's house in the afternoon. Hannah was already there and we chilled out for a couple of hours, playing pool and talking rubbish. Hannah was trying to get us to think about stuff for the next school paper but we ignored her. Grace was in her usual weirdo mood, talking about rabbits and their poo.

'They eat their own poo,' she said, just as I was about to sink the black ball and beat Jit's sad ass for the fifth time. It put me right off my shot and the ball cannoned off three cushions.

'Eurgh!' I said.

'That's nasty man . . .' added Jit, screwing up his face.

'They do, though,' said Grace, grinning.

'No they don't,' replied Hannah. 'I used to have one – I know . . .'

'You obviously don't,' said Grace. 'Rabbits have something like seventeen thousand taste glands or something and humans only have ten thousand . . .'

'Easy, Sister Gee,' I said. 'You sound like you're doin' a documentary.'

'It's true. When they poo some of the nutrients and stuff are still in it and they eat it to get the rest out . . .'

'Man, that's why I ain't *never* havin' no pets,' said Jit.

'Duttyness,' I said.

'I used to kiss my bunny,' said Hannah.

'*NAH! You dutty raas!*' I shouted.

'Not *really*,' said Hannah, getting embarrassed and trying to ride it out.

'You're *gonna* say that now,' Jit told her. 'You is feelin' *shame*.'

'I was *joking*,' she replied.

'Hannah kiss the bunny with botty breath . . . *nah*!' I continued, until Hannah picked up a spare cue and came towards me.

'Easy, Sister Aitch, I was only playing,' I said, pretending to be scared.

'I'm gonna shove this up your ar—'

'Well, this is becoming rather familiar,' said Mr Parkhurst from the foot of the stairs.

Hannah looked at him and said, 'Oh my God.'

'You seem to have a thing about Dean and that cue,' said Mr Parkhurst.

The rest of us cracked up while Hannah went red. Again.

'Anyone fancy a coffee?' asked Grace's dad.

'*Yeah*!' said Jit, like a little kid. 'Can I help you make it?'

'Of course you can, Jit,' replied Mr Parkhurst.

Jit followed him upstairs as Grace turned to me and Hannah and mimicked her dad.

'*Of course you can Jit – why not lick my bum while you're at it?*' she whispered in a childish voice.

'Like Hannah and the bunny?' I said.

'*DEAN*!' shouted Hannah, grabbing the cue again.

We all went for a walk about an hour later, after Grace's dad made us promise to stay for tea. We walked down past a row of shops on a road called Francis Street and then cut across to the main road that led into the city. From there we walked down a side street and eventually reached Queens Road where we stopped at a shop to buy chocolate because Grace said that she would die if she didn't have some. Jit waited outside for us and when we returned he looked amazed.

'What?' I asked him.

'You look like someone just shot you,' said Hannah.

'Look over the road,' said Jit, pointing to a newsagent's.

'*What*?' asked Grace. 'It's a shop . . .'

'They're *in* the shop,' said Jit.

'Who, gimpy boy?' asked Hannah.

'Imi and Suky,' replied Jit.

'Ooh, cool,' said Grace. 'I need to talk to Suky about some homework.'

'*Nah*,' said Jit, 'you don't get me. They're in there together . . .'

'So?' I asked, starting to get bored.

'*TOGETHER* . . . like, holding hands . . .' he replied.

'*NO!*' said Grace and Hannah together.

'Yep – seen them with my own eyes, man. They were holding hands.'

Hannah and Grace grabbed us and pulled us back into the shop we had just come out of.

'What you doin' you divs?' I shouted.

'*SSSH!*' said Grace. 'They'll hear you when they come out.'

'And?'

'God, boys. We *don't* want them to *see* us,' said Hannah, like that was supposed to make sense.

'Let's follow them . . .' said Grace.

'No, let's do something really interesting like watch our feet grow,' said Jit.

'Oh shut up, farty pants,' said Grace.

'*Oh my God there they are!*' said Hannah, as though she'd seen a movie star.

'*Hide!*' said Grace, pulling me and Jit further back into the shop, just as an old man was trying to get out. He tut-tutted at us and walked off mumbling.

'Stupid old man,' said Grace.

Across the street Imi and Suky walked up towards some traffic lights. They didn't have a clue that they were being watched and they didn't look like they cared, holding hands and stopping to kiss each other every few moments. It was like something out of a chick flick. Grace waited until they had turned a corner before walking out of the shop.

'Come on . . .' she said to the rest of us. 'Let's see where they go . . .'

We spent the next hour and a half following Imi and Suky, as they walked in some kind of strange zigzag pattern back towards the area they lived in, which was near Grace's house. They took the long way round to everywhere and a couple of times we had to duck and hide behind hedges and stuff so that they wouldn't spot us. At first it was OK because it was like we were on a secret mission or something but eventually it just got really boring and I was getting hungry too. So was Jit, who moaned all the way like he was a five-year-old, which was also the way that Grace and Hannah were acting. They were giggling to each other and talking about how they were going to tease Suky on Monday.

'She told us that she thought he was *ugly*,' said Hannah.

'To put you off her trail, prob'ly,' I replied.

'Cheeky moo,' said Grace. 'And *he* said that he didn't fancy her at all – the little liar . . .'

'What did you expect them to say with you two witches on their case? I don't get what the big deal is, myself . . .' I replied.

'Idiot,' said Hannah, matter-of-factly. 'It's all about group dynamics . . .'

'Is that food?' asked Jit. 'Only I'm gonna faint if I don't eat soon.'

'No one,' began Grace, ignoring Jit, 'in our little group has crossed the line between friendship and romance until now. It's bound to change the way things work . . .'

'How we all relate to each other,' added Hannah.

'You been reading too many of them stupid magazines,' I said. 'I'm not gonna start bein' different with you two just because them two can't stop lick each other's faces . . .'

'Yeah,' said Jit, before looking at Grace and then looking away. I don't know why he was trying to take my side. It was obvious he was mad about Grace.

'See what we mean?' said Hannah.

'Nah . . .' I lied.

'So it'll be you and Hannah, soon enough,' said Grace, winking at Jit.

'Leave it,' said Hannah.

'Get off that, man. You'd love to go out with me – I am the dan . . . how many times you gotta hear it, sista.'

As Suky and Imi got closer to their own area they let go of each other's hands and started to act normally again. We followed them right up to Imi's road and then we turned and headed back for Grace's house. Someone was going to get maximum grief on Monday, I thought to myself, before I let my mind fill with the images of food. Fat cheeseburgers with mustard and ketchup, greasy fried chicken and chips with hot pepper sauce, lamb kebabs like the ones from Picnic Kebab House on Evington Road, packed with salad and chillis and that fried Haloumi cheese thing that my mum gets from the supermarket. Only when we got to Grace's it was vegetable lasagne and home made garlic bread. Not that I was complaining though. I was so hungry I would have eaten Jit if I could.

THIRTEEN

The following Monday Grace wasn't at the bus stop when me and Jit got there and when we got to school she was already gossiping about Imi and Suky with everyone in our class. Suky and Imi weren't there when we arrived. They'd been sent to pick up some stuff for Mrs Dooher and when they returned everyone went quiet for a moment. Then Marco and Milorad whistled and the whole class went mad. Imi went red and sat down but Suky stood where she was, looking confused.

'You got seen!' shouted Puspha, talking to Suky.

'All kissy face and holding hands,' added Heather, as Dilip and Raj turned to face Imi.

'*Nah* . . . Imi's got a *girlfriend*!' they said, like little girls.

I didn't get what the big deal was. If they wanted to check each other then that was cool with me – I mean we were getting old and that. The problem was, as my sister once told me, that some of us were more mature than the others and Dilip and Raj were like, six, compared to me. The knobs.

'Did you hold her hand?' asked Raj, grinning.

'Did she kiss you first or was it the other way round?' asked Heather.

'All right, all right . . . You sound like you're doing a rehearsal of Grease,' said Mrs Dooher. She had a little smile on her face when she said it.

'What's Grease?' asked Marco.

'You've got it all over your face, you dutty raas,' said Jit.

'*Miss*!' squealed Marco.

'*SHUT UP*!' shouted Mrs Dooher.

Everyone quietened down but they were still whispering to each other as Mrs Dooher took the register. I turned to Imi and smiled. 'Nice one, bro, although you could have let me know . . .' I told him.

'Shut up, Dean,' replied Imi, looking well pissed off.

'Nah . . . I ain't joking. If you and Suky wanna bump uglies – that's none of my business, man . . .'

'How did the *whole* class find out anyway?' he asked me.

'You'll have to ask the blabber mouth girlies,' I told him, nodding towards Hannah and Grace who were talking to Suky and giggling again.

'I should have known,' he said, before smiling.

'So you two serious and that?' I asked.

'S'pose,' he replied.

'You kept that quiet,' added Jit, joining in.

'That's because I knew that if I said anything the whole school would find out about it,' he told us.

'So what? Ain't like you should care . . .' I said.

'I don't. I just could have done without all the gossip,' said Imi, acting all mature. Like he'd never gossiped about anyone.

'Your parents mind that she's Sikh and you is Muslim?' asked Jit.

Imi shrugged.

'You ain't told 'em,' I said, 'I bet you let go of her hand when you reach the end of your road and that . . .'

Imi gave me a funny look, 'NO!' he said, defensively. 'What you know about it anyway?'

'I just do,' said Jit. 'There's that whole family honour thing, ain't there?'

'Not with my family,' said Imi.

'Least not until you tell 'em,' I said, grinning.

'Suky's family might not like it,' he said.

'Really?' I asked but he turned away and shrugged.

'You'll have to ask her, bro,' he told me, like he'd said too much.

'I gettit – it's cool,' I told him.

'Can we talk about something else?' asked Imi, looking at Jit.

'Yep,' said Jit. 'How about rabbits?'

'You *what*?'

'*Rabbits*, man. They eat their own shit,' replied Jit, smiling.

Imi looked at me and then back at Jit. 'You two need to get a life,' he said.

'Maybe a girlfriend too,' grinned Jit.

It went on and on like that all morning with Jit taking every opportunity to return to the same subject. In the end it got boring and at lunch I walked off to see if I could find Misha, who was in the year above us and *fine*. I wanted to get her phone number but didn't have the guts to ask for it. Not that I got the chance. I was walking down the main corridor in school, heading for the rear of the building when Dilip caught up with me.

'Bro,' he called out.

I turned and saw him standing behind me, looking sheepish.

'Easy, Dilip,' I said.

'Got a problem, innit?' he told me.

'Yeah?' I replied.

'Them tings gone funny,' he said.

'You what?'

'Them phones gone barred . . .'

For a minute I was about to smile but then what he said sunk in and I felt my stomach knot.

The phones were dodgy and I'd spent all the money on turntables.

I stood and thought quickly, before trying to talk my way out of it.

'Sold as seen,' I told him.

'Huh?' said Dilip, looking confused.

'Like when you buy stuff at a car boot sale, man. No refunds, my brother.'

'But it don't work,' he said, his voice breaking a bit.

'Ain't my fault,' I said, trying to act brave.

Secretly though I was feeling bad. I mean I liked selling stuff and making money but I wasn't a con man or nothing. I wouldn't have sold the phones if I'd known that they didn't work. And that's when I remembered Gussie saying '*that's the least I can do . . .*' after I'd asked to use his Switch card. The *wanker*.

'I w . . . want my money b . . . back,' stammered Dilip.

'No way, Jose,' I said. 'I ain't got it no more . . .'

'But . . .'

I had to think quickly so I said the first thing that came into my head.

'Tell you what – let me talk to my mate Raj tonight. I'll get him to sort them out – can't say fairer than that . . .'

Dilip looked at me and shrugged.

'OK,' he said.

'I didn't know they was dodgy,' I told him. 'Honestly, bro. I wouldn't do that.'

'You gonna speak to Raj then?' he asked.

'I just said so, didn't I? Check me tomorrow and I'll sort it,' I said, walking away in a real hurry.

I walked out of the school and across a concrete square over to one of the other buildings, ignoring Misha and her mates. I didn't have time for chatting up no sisters. I had to think quick. I walked through the door and headed for the toilets. Pushing open the door, I saw Paresh Solanki at the mirror, straightening his greasy hair.

'I wanna talk to you, Dean,' he said to me.

'Get lost Paresh,' I said. 'I got things to do . . .'

He pulled out one of the phones.

'Yeah, you have. Like giving me back my money for this phone,' he said.

I looked at him as though he was holding a stick of dynamite or something. I hadn't sold him a phone.

'Where'd you get that?' I asked.

'Dilip got it for me,' he said.

'I didn't know you and Dilip was mates,' I said.

'Cousins,' he told me.

'Well, like I just told him – I'm sorting it out later. Check me tomorrow and I'll get it unbarred . . .'

Paresh came closer to me.

'You better,' he said.

Even though he was older than me I wasn't scared of him. It's not like he was Jason Patel. And then I remembered the phone that Jason took.

'You listening to me?' asked Paresh.

'Yeah, yeah,' I replied, trying not to let my fear show on my face. Jason was going to go mad – even though he'd never paid for the phone. I just knew what he was like.

'I'll find you tomorrow, then,' said Paresh, walking out into the corridor.

I sat in a cubicle after he'd gone and thought about how I was going to murder my brother. Then, as the bell went for the afternoon lessons, I sneaked my way through the school, praying that I didn't bump into Jason or anyone else that I'd sold a phone to. I made it to my next lesson in one piece and sat quietly at the back as Mrs Lee-Cross tried to explain something about fractions. The only fractions on my mind were the ones I'd be in when Jason got hold of me. I sneaked to my last lesson too, using Jit as cover and I explained what was going on. Jit looked worried.

'But I ain't got the money no more,' he said.

'I know . . . but that ain't gonna help us.'

'Your brother should sort it out – it's his fault . . .' said Jit.

'Oh believe it,' I said. 'Man, when I get home I'm gonna go mad . . .'

'He'll have to get Raj to sort 'em out,' said Jit.

'Yeah – only Raj is gonna charge twenty pound a phone, minimum . . .'

'Shit – I didn't think of that,' said Jit.

'And we ain't got the money... the decks, remember...?'

'Can't we cancel the order?' asked Jit.

I shook my head.

'They're getting delivered today, They's probably already at my house...'

'Raas...' replied Jit.

I didn't tell him about Jason though and I knew that Jason was going to be my biggest headache. After school I was standing with Imi and Jit, waiting for the bus when the inevitable happened.

'*OI*! *DEAN*...!' came Jason's voice, just as the bus was pulling up and it started to rain. I was about to get on board but realised that Jason would catch up and get on too. In the end my only hope was to do a runner.

'*I'm gone*...!' I told Jit and Imi who had just bought their tickets.

I jumped through the open doors, past the other kids and splashed through the heavy rain, running as fast as I could. I could hear Jason shouting after me as I ran, my heart pounding...

FOURTEEN

'You looked like a drowned rat,' said my brother, as I stood shivering in the doorway to our living room.

'There's only one rat round here, bro,' I replied, giving him the dirtiest screw face I could manage.

'What's up wit' you?' he asked.

I dumped my bag on the floor and rubbed my hand across my wet head.

'You ain't got *no* shame, have you?'

Gussie, who'd been lying on the sofa in front of the telly, sat up and scratched his head.

'The phones?' I said.

'Oh . . . yeah I was gonna . . .' he began but I didn't give him the chance to finish what he was saying.

'You *knew* them phones was dodgy and you let me sell 'em. Now I've gotta get them all sorted and I've spent the dough on decks and you knew all the time that they was . . .'

'They came,' said Gussie.

'*WHAT?*' I asked him, getting angrier.

'The decks, bro. They arrived this morning. I've even set them up for you and everything . . .'

'I don't give a toss 'bout the decks, man. You ripped me off. I'm your *brother* . . .'

Gussie shrugged and then grinned at me.

'No worries, bro. I'll speak to Raj . . .' he said.

'I'm gonna get *murdered* when I get back to school and all you can do is smile at me, you t'ief . . .'

He gave me a funny look.

'Who's gonna murder you?' he said.

'This lad at school, Jason Patel, took one of the phones and I've just had to run all the way home 'cause he was after me and I'm gonna get battered and all you can do is . . .' I said, running out of breath before I could finish.

'Ease up, rude bwoi . . . ain't no one gonna batter you,' said my brother. 'Who's this Jason Patel anyway?'

'Just some lad from Year Ten . . .'

'Well forget about him – if he touches you I'll break his legs . . .'

'What about the rest of 'em? They all want their money back, man,' I said.

Gussie grinned again.

'I'll sort it,' he told me. 'I'm sorry, man. Raj told me they was OK . . .'

'That's why you let me have them for next to nothing, is it?' I was glaring at him.

'All right – so I knew that they might get barred but I didn't—'

'You're bang out of order,' I said.

'And you sound like your lines was written by someone on *EastEnders*,' he replied.

'Go stick your head . . .'

'Leave it, bro. I said I'll sort it out. Let me give Raj a call.'

He pulled out his mobile and dialled a number, gesturing to a bag by his feet.

'Computer software . . . graphics and games and stuff. I got 'em for you to sell . . .' he said, before talking to whoever answered the phone.

As he went through it all with Raj I looked at the software and then went to find a towel to dry off with. I was feeling a bit better, especially after Gussie had said that he'd take care of Jason but I was still recovering from being chased half the way home and I wasn't about to forget that my own brother had ripped me off. I walked back into the living room to find Gussie lying down again.

'*So?*' I asked.

'Sorted . . . he's gonna take the bar off 'em. Just tell whoever you sold them to that he'll do it for a tenner . . .'

'But they ain't gonna go for that,' I said. 'They've already paid for them.'

'They's still getting a *bargain*, man. Them things are pure top dollar . . .'

'But I'm gonna get beat up,' I said.

'Tell them that it's better than a kick in the teeth which is what they'll get if they touch you.'

'But . . .' I began.

Gussie shook his head at me. 'You tell them man that if they wanna get funny they can come see me. Tell 'em that I've got their money . . .'

I thought about it for a moment and then nodded.

'OK . . .' I said.

'And meanwhile you can off load them CDs in the bag . . . keep the money.'

'What's wrong with them?' I asked, learning my lesson fast.

'Nothing, man. It's just software, you get me?'

'But no one's gonna want it . . .'

'You ain't even tried yet,' said Gussie.

'But . . .'

'Man, just get out of my face. I've sorted out the phones – what else you want? Go play on your decks or summat.'

I mumbled a few swear words under my breath and went up to my room. When I saw the decks I cheered up a bit and thought about calling for Jit. He'd want to know why I had run off anyway and besides we had the turntables to play with. I even forgot about Jason as I put on a tune that I borrowed from Gussie's collection, a ragga thing by Capleton. I went and called for Jit about an hour after dinner and we spent ages on the decks, as I told him all about why Jason had chased me. In the end I stopped worrying, remembering what Gussie had said about sorting him out. But if I thought that my troubles were over, I was wrong.

I made it to school the next morning without Jit, who didn't turn up at the stop again. I made it without seeing anyone that had bought one of the phones, too. Then again, I *did* have my hood up all the way to school and didn't take it down until I reached the safety of my form room. Jason was still out to get me and Gussie couldn't help me in school so I still had to be careful. I saw Dilip and told him all about the deal with Raj, and to begin with he wasn't having any of it.

'Nah, bro – I paid the money already,' he whispered, as Mrs Dooher called the register.

I remembered what Gussie had said to me and repeated it. 'You're still getting the bargain of the century, man. It's only another tenner . . .'

'I dunno man . . .'

'Well if you want your dough back you need to go see my brother . . .' I told him.

It did the trick. He mumbled something about never buying anything from me again and turned his back on me. But I prodded his shoulder so that he'd turn back around.

'And tell Paresh too. If he wants to get tough he can do it with my bro, man, you get me?'

Dilip went red and turned away again. I didn't feel pleased though. It wasn't my fault that the phones were dodgy and I didn't want to piss off my school mates. I didn't want them going round telling everyone that I was shady and that. That was the kind of reputation I could do without.

'What you talkin' 'bout, sexy boy?' asked Grace.

'Nuttin',' I said, lying.

'I didn't realise that you and Dilip were such good friends . . .' she said.

'We're not.'

'Oh . . . must be my imagination,' said Grace, grinning.

The door slammed open and Jit hurried in, looking like he had been dragged through a hedge backwards.

'Yes, scarecrow!' said Imi, as Jit sat down.

'Jit . . . can I see you after registration,' said Mrs Dooher, not even looking up from what she was doing.

'Oops,' said Hannah.

'What up wit' you?' I asked him.

'Jus' late,' he said.

One side of his face looked a bit swollen. Grace noticed, too.

'Someone hit you?' she asked, looking all concerned.

Jit looked at me and shrugged.

'Jason,' he said. 'He told me to give you a message . . .'

'Why would Jason hit—' began Hannah.

'Nuttin',' I said. 'We'll sort it out later.'

I gave Jit a look that said don't talk about it anymore and he nodded at me.

'You boys are silly,' Grace told us. 'That's twice in two weeks that Jason's beat up Jit. Just tell someone . . .'

'Don't worry,' I said, angrily. 'I'm going to – Just as soon as I see that bwoi myself . . .'

'Ooh hard man,' laughed Hannah.

'Just watch this space, Sister Aitch,' I replied.

FIFTEEN

I didn't see Jason for a couple of days although I did have to fend off grief about the phones from the other people I'd sold them to. No one was happy about having to pay extra to get them to work apart from the bloke who owned the phone shop I reckon but I managed to get out of it pretty easily. The problem was that everyone found out about the dodgy phones which meant that I was having serious trouble selling anything else. All my usual customers were keeping well away and every time I saw Dilip he just ignored me and whispered stuff to his mates. I was like a leper. Kids were avoiding me in the corridor and pointing at me when I walked past but it wasn't all to do with the phones. Eventually Hannah told me that she'd overheard some of the lads in our class talking about me.

'They said that Jason is after your blood,' she said, looking worried.

I tried to shrug it off. 'He's always after me or Jit — nothing new there, sister.'

'This is serious, Dean. Those lads were laughing and

talking about how Jason has been spreading it around that he's going to batter you . . .'

I still hadn't asked Gussie for help and I wondered whether the time had come to do just that. Only, I knew that I'd get called a grass if I did. People would think that I couldn't take care of myself and that would mean that the other bullies in school would start to pick on me too. At least that's what I thought. I decided that it would all blow over anyway. I hadn't seen Jason so he couldn't have been that bothered, I said to myself. I was wrong about that too, though.

'You're nuts,' Hannah told me.

'Let him come,' I said, trying to act all hard. 'He don't bother me.'

She shook her head at me.

'One of these days,' she replied, 'you're going to get yourself into something that you can't talk your way out of . . .'

I grinned. 'Never. I could talk my way out of anything . . . Besides, them bullies *want* you to be scared of 'em. They don't like it when you aren't. Them can't tek it.'

'I still don't understand *why* he's after you though,' said Hannah, as Grace walked up.

'Who's after who?' she asked.

'Jason. He's telling people that he's going to beat Dean up.'

'Do you want me to knee him where it hurts?' asked Grace, jokingly.

'I wish that would help,' I admitted.

'So, why is he after you?' asked Hannah.

'Nuttin' really – just some stuff about a phone that don't work.'

I told them the whole story. After I'd finished Grace shook her head at me.

'You aren't supposed to do that at school anyway,' she told me.

'Who cares?' I replied.

'Dean . . . at least be a bit more serious. Jason is a nasty piece of work,' she told me.

'Yeah,' added Hannah. 'I don't want my favourite boy getting beaten up over something so silly . . .'

'Easy,' I replied, grinning. 'So now I'm your favourite boy?'

'You know what I mean,' said Hannah. 'Stop being an arse.'

'But what about Jit?' I continued. 'He'll be jealous . . .'

'See what I mean?' said Hannah, looking pissed off. 'Stupid boy . . .'

'Silly, macho, too much testosterone in your pants, smelly rabbit poo eating boy,' added Grace.

'Take a breath, Sister Gee,' I told her. 'You'll do yourself some damage . . .'

They told me to get lost and walked off together. I just stood and shook my heads. Girls are some funny things, man.

Jit wasn't around when I caught the bus home and I spent the journey wondering where he had got to. As the bus turned down Evington Road I watched a group of kids make their way downstairs, ready to get off at the next stop. Mine was further up the road, just before the bus headed into the city centre but I decided to get off early so that I could go to the shops. It was beginning to rain as I got off, jumping past Marco and Milorad.

'Watch it!' said Marco.

'Sorry bro,' I replied, skidding on the wet pavement and colliding with Misha and one of her friends.

'Stupid knob!' shouted her mate, but Misha just stood and grinned at me.

'Hey Misha – what you doin'?' I asked, stupidly.

'Whaddya think I'm doin'?' she replied, still smiling.

'Goin' home?'

'That's what I usually do after school . . .'

'Oh right. So, like, what are you . . .' I began again, not really knowing what I was going to say.

'This bwoi stupid, y'know,' said Misha's mate.

'No I ain't,' I said.

The girl held her hand in my face, just like my sister does, and turned her head away.

'Fool . . .' she said.

'Did you wanna ask me something, Dean?' said Misha.

I did. I wanted her phone number but my stomach knotted up and I couldn't think of anything to say. Nothing clever anyway.

'Er . . .'

'See?' said her friend. 'Stupid bwoi cyaan even talk properly . . .'

They walked off giggling and left me standing in the rain with my ego seriously bruised. I was the lyrics officer, man and I couldn't even ask the girl for her digits. I needed to have serious chat with myself.

I didn't feel bad for too long though. I crossed the road, running around the cars that were held up in a traffic jam and walked into an off-licence.

'Twenny B&H,' I said to the man behind the counter, as a joke.

'You know you ain't old enough,' said the bloke, whose name was Hardev.

'OK – you got me, bro. I'll just take a gallon of Vodka and ten cigars . . .'

Hardev smiled and shook his head. 'You gonna buy anything, Dean?'

I nodded. 'Yeah, man. Just you looked kinda bored so

I thought I'd come cheer you up,' I said.

'Buy the shop and let me go live on a beach somewhere,' replied Hardev, who had gone to school with my brother.

'How much you want? I got one pound and twenty-three old English pennies in me hand . . .' I told him.

He grinned again.

'Get out of it you likkle raas . . .'

I picked up a bar of chocolate and gave him the right money.

'What kind of way is that to treat your best customer?' I said.

'I'll give you the back of my hand in a minute,' said Hardev, as I walked out the door.

The chocolate went down in two mouthfuls and as I crossed East Park Road, I decided that I wanted another one. There was a twenty-four hour shop further up the road and I walked in, past a couple of fit student girls, and headed for the sweet aisle. As I turned into it though I came face to face with the dog's backside that made up Jason Patel's face.

'Who we got here then?' he said, smiling.

I didn't stop to think. I grabbed a handful of chocolates and shoved them in his face pushing him into a display. He went flying and as I ran out the guy behind the counter and the security guard swore in an African language and went mad. I took a right down the side of the shop and headed up the street. Behind me I heard Jason swearing and realised that he was on my tail. I ducked left into the second side street and sprinted for the top of it, where it joined St Stephen's Road. Jason was still behind me as I ran across the main road and on into Guilford Street, where I could have ducked left and towards my own house.

Instead, like a complete knob, I went the other way and found myself being closed in on by a really mad looking Jason. He was calling me all kinds of names and people were stopping to watch what was going on, not a single one of them doing anything to help me. Then I saw a little kid, about three, right in my path. He was only a few yards away and I couldn't stop. I would have knocked him down. Instead, I picked him up and then came to a stop. Behind us his mother shouted after me from the front door of their house. I turned and ran back with the kid, who was grinning at me, and handed him over. I mumbled sorry and then I heard Jason hit a wheelie-bin. I turned and ran on, beginning to laugh to myself like a mad man, even though I was bricking it.

I sprinted down another road with big tall Victorian houses on both sides and on past the entrance to a synagogue. I had to stop and catch my breath a bit then and when I turned I could see Jason, still coming after me and holding some kind of stick in his hands. I set off again, down College Street which is really narrow and has these alleyways on both sides. I ran past a blonde girl walking a fat Rottweiller, not stopping even though she had smiled at me, and then I turned into Prebend Street where I nearly knocked over a policeman.

'Hold on, mate . . .' said the copper, grabbing me by the jacket.

'Lemme go, man!'

'Calm down . . . what are you running away from?' he said, all suspicious.

I pushed his hands away and caught my breath.

'Someone's after me,' I said. 'With a stick . . .' I pointed round the corner and the policeman went to have a look.

'No one here mate,' he told me.

'But he was *right* behind me,' I said, walking back round the corner.

The street was empty except for the blonde girl who was trying to drag her dog behind her and she was up near the top of the road.

'No one at all . . .' said the policeman.

'Must have seen you and done a runner,' I said.

'Would you like to make a report?' he asked but I shook my head.

'Right, well try and be more careful next time – you could have hurt me,' he said.

I looked at him like he was mad.

'Ain't that your job?' I asked. 'Anything to protect the tax paying public?'

He gave me a really dirty look in return.

'Gotta be off,' I said. 'Me mum's made bacon sandwiches for tea . . .' And I ran off again before he had the chance to grab my jacket again.

By the time I got in I was soaked again and I'd decided that enough was enough. It was time to tell my brother that I needed his help. I walked into the living room expecting to see Gussie lying around on his fat arse as usual. He wasn't in though. My sister was sitting where he normally sat, watching the telly and talking to a friend on the phone at the same time.

'Ooh *yeah*,' she said, into the handset.

'You see Gussie?' I asked.

She gave me a dirty look, covered the mouthpiece with her hand and told me that she was trying to have a conversation.

'Just tell me where Gussie is,' I replied.

'He's out . . . what am I – his *mum*?' she said before turning to her conversation *and* turning up the volume on the telly. Girls . . .

SIXTEEN

The next day I found Jit talking to Robert and Wesley at lunch. They were in the computer room with Hannah, Grace, Imi and Suky, and the fantasy twins were *still* talking about that book.

'Princess Wondlebarn used the Shield of Ages to deflect the magic powers of Gerafaggan,' Robert was saying when I joined them.

'And she released Tar from the Dark Way too,' added Wesley.

'So the people of Nebilet are free from the evils of Gerafaggan . . .' continued Robert.

'What – *for ever?*' I asked, with a smile.

'Well – Gerafaggan *has* escaped into the Void with the Flute of Kings so I assume that there will be a sequel . . .' replied Robert.

'Oh I should hope so,' said Wesley.

'What *void?*' asked Jit.

'The Void is the no man's land between the evil forces and those of the Lighted Path,' Robert explained.

Jit just looked more confused than ever.

'Hang on . . . you never told me nothing about no Lighted Path . . .' he said.

'It's there at the very beginning of the book when Time speaks to Princess Wondlebarn and warns her of the evil machinations of her wicked uncle, Gerafaggan, and his dastardly wife, Noreanna . . .' explained Wesley.

'Sounds like you're making it all up to me,' I said.

Wesley pulled the book from his bag. It was about three times the thickness of a normal book and had a painting on the cover of warlocks and winged horses and a blonde princess with flowing locks. Boring . . .

'There you go,' he said. 'You may borrow it if you like – I'm already reading another.'

'What's the new one about?' I asked, instantly wishing that I hadn't.

'It's the prequel to this one – *Gerafaggan the Glorious*,' said Wesley.

'Man – this is just mad. How many *are* there?' I asked.

'Seven so far,' said Robert. 'The author is writing the eighth as we speak . . .'

'What *right* now?' asked Jit.

'I shouldn't be surprised,' replied Robert.

'Nah – them authors got an easy life, you get me? I bet the author's sitting on his arse looking out the window and drinking coffee and that . . .' said Jit.

I yawned real loud to show him that I was bored of the conversation and headed over to where Hannah was seated at a computer, her fingers tapping away at the keyboard.

'Yo, Sister Aitch, what you doin'?' I asked.

'Working,' she said, not even looking up.

Jit came over and asked me if I'd told Gussie about Jason yet. I told him about Jason chasing after me and about how I hadn't seen Gussie yet.

'I'm going to though,' I said. 'I've had enough of that knob chasing me around with his piggy eyes and butt for a face . . .'

'Cool – it's about time Gussie taught him some manners anyways,' replied Jit.

'Too right,' I said.

'Man's a dickhead . . .' added Jit, as Robert coughed in the way that you do when you want someone to look at you. I ignored him.

'Looks like a monkey anyway,' I said. 'With his red hair and mash-up mout' and that . . .'

I heard the cough again and then Hannah and Grace took a deep breath, at the same time, like they were joined at the hip or something. I turned to see what Robert wanted and came face to face for the second time in twenty-four hours with Jason Patel.

'*Er . . .*' I began.

'I wanna talk to you,' he said. 'Outside, in the corridor . . .'

I waited for the punch but it never came. I followed Jason out of the room, telling Jit that I'd be all right on my own. It was time to face up to him anyway, I thought to myself. I had to stand up to him, beating or not. I was sick of his bullying.

He turned to me in the corridor and tried to smile. Then I saw the bruises on his face for the first time. Out of the corner of my eye I could see the others pressed up against the glass, all looking worried.

'I got to say summat,' he said, quietly.

'What?' I asked. 'Ain't even like you *paid* for that phone so I don't see how you can ask for no money back . . .'

'I . . . you . . . the phone is yours . . .'

'You *what*?'

'You can have the phone, bro. I just wanted to say that . . . well . . . that I'm kinda s . . . s . . . sorry and that.'

I looked at him for a minute, expecting to see his ugly grin break on his face and for a left hook to come flying in but he just stood where he was, looking at the floor. It was then that I realised that he was actually apologising to me for real. Jason Patel, bully boy number one, saying sorry like he was six and had been caught stealing sweets by his mum. Man, I wanted to laugh. 'If I've ever upset you . . . you know bullied you and that . . . I was wrong, bro and well . . .' he continued.

'*What?*' I asked, much more confident now.

'If you ever need anyt'ing or anyone has a go at you . . . just come to me and I'll . . .'

'Man, you're takin' the piss,' I said. I couldn't believe what I was hearing. The man was chasing me round the streets only a few hours earlier and now he was all sheepish and that.

Maybe I'm a bit stupid or maybe I just didn't realise that it was a possibility but I finally worked it out and grinned to myself.

'Anyway, I gave the phone to your brother last night . . .' he said.

'So, you *met* Gussie then . . . ?' I asked, smirking. Well, *you* would have.

'Er . . . *yeah*. Anyway I gotta go, man . . . laters.'

And with that he walked away. I stood where I was for a while, just letting it all sink in. How had Gussie known where to find him anyway and what had he said? Man, my mind was in overdrive. I headed back into the class, smiling.

'What was all *that* about?' asked Grace.

'*Yeah* – what did he want?' added Jit.

'Oh, nuttin' – just wanted to *apologise* to me . . .' I replied.

'*Get lost!*' said Jit. 'What did he *really* want?'

I shrugged.

'Dunno – just some shit about them phones . . . nuttin' serious.'

'But he said he was going to beat you up,' said Hannah.

'Maybe he had a change of heart . . . like, you know, maybe he ran out of *guss* . . .' I said with a grin.

'You mean *gas*,' corrected Grace.

'Hey, posh chick – I know what I mean . . .'

Jit looked at me, grinned and shook his head and then he turned back to Robert and Wesley.

'I got this idea, man . . . *Ganglefart the Goblin and the Witches of Devana* . . . Hannah and Grace is the witches . . .'

When I got home that night, Gussie was in the kitchen with Gramps, reading a newspaper.

'Anything you want to tell me, bro?' I asked, as I sat down.

He grinned.

'*Nah*,' he said, shaking his head. 'Nuttin' really springs to mind . . .'

'You *sure* now?'

'Yeah . . . Oh no, hang on a minute. There *was* this skinny-arsed kid I seen last night running away from some school bully like he was running for his life . . .'

'You *seen* me?' I asked, amazed.

'So I thought I'd maybe pull the bully up, y'know. Teach him a likkle lesson and that . . . he was only *too* keen to listen to me. And he gave me a likkle something to give to the poor kid he was chasing.' He pulled the phone from his pocket and set it down in front of me.

Now it was my turn to grin and I did, so wide that my Gramps raised an eyebrow at me.

'Yuh ago crack yuh face bwoi, grinnin' like yuh a win de sweepstake dung a Caymanas . . .'

'Where?' I asked.

'It's a race track in Kingston,' Gussie told me.

'Oh right . . .'

'Anything you gotta say to me, bro?' he asked.

'Yeah,' I said. 'Next time make sure you get proper gear to sell . . .'

'Yuh cheeky raas . . .' he replied.

'One time, back in sixty-three,' said Gramps, 'me tek dat bwoi Bob Marley dung de track. Dat bwoi a gamble off alla him money pon one stupid 'orse name GullyRat and den 'em waan my money too . . . !' He chuckled to himself at the memory, real or not.

'You what?' I asked, wondering what the hell Gramps was on about.

'Is a nice phone yuh have deh, bwoi, you wan' sell it?' he said, forgetting what he had just been talking about, as usual.

For a *moment* I considered it. *Just* for a moment but then I shook my head.

'Nah, Gramps. It don't work anyway . . .'

Gramps shrugged, farted and then shook his head. I wasn't about to sell the dodgy phone to him or anyone else. I'd learnt my lesson. From now on I was going to check anything I sold, myself. I mean, I didn't want to end up on one of them consumer programmes like the Watchdog or nothing. I got up and went to use the land line, calling Jit.

'Wanna come over for dinner?' I asked.

'Yeah, man,' he replied.

'You may as well bring your stuff too. You know we're gonna be messing with them decks 'til whenever, anyway . . .'

'Cool,' said Jit.

I put the phone down and turned to my Gramps.

'You still got all them old tunes in your room, Gramps?' I asked him.

'Yeah man – why?' he replied, smiling.

'Wanna play me some of them . . . *y'know*, educate de yout' dem . . .'

'Well, alright,' said Gramps. 'But any more of yuh cheek and yuh ago get . . .'

'Yeah I know Gramps . . . *lick dung*!'

I ran before his well aimed cuff could catch my ears.